The Visiting Professor

THE COLLEGE ROUTE SERIES
BOOK THREE

DENISE ESSEX

#BLP

Heart Piercing Swoon Worthy Black Love Stories

Visit bit.ly/readBLP to join our mailing list for sneak peeks and release day links!

B. Love Publications - where Authors celebrate black men, black women, and black love.

To submit a manuscript for consideration, email your first three chapters to blovepublications@gmail.com with SUBMISSION as the subject.

The BLP Podcast – bit.ly/BLPUncovered

Let's connect on social media!
Facebook - B. Love Publications
Twitter - @blovepub
Instagram - @blovepublications

For Sophia

I also dedicate this book to anyone in recovery, be it officially or on your own. I see you!

Acknowledgments

I'd like to thank:
My family: Thank you for your support of my writing career.
My publisher and the dopest pen sisters an author could ask for:
Thank you for your advice, support, and encouragement.
CYN: I told you before, you are a magician. Thank you!
Editors and proofreaders: Angels sent from heaven. Y'all dope AF!
Special shout out to Latisha! Thank you for your patience and all the
invaluable information you share!
Me: Thank you for *continuing* to do it, despite your fears.
Readers: Thank you for taking time from your life to play in my world!

Introduction

Dear reader,

Thank you for your interest in my current release. This book features a brief discussion of childhood physical abuse. Please take care of yourself if you find this topic triggering. If you resonate with what you read, please leave a positive review on Amazon, and share it with your friends.

With Love,
Denise Essex

Prologue

VERONICA

I SCROLLED my smart phone like a lunatic. Rashad had dumped me months ago, but I'd convinced myself he'd eventually crawl back to me. I kept working out. My hair and makeup... flawless. I stayed in places I knew he'd be to ensure I was visible. Rashad belonged to me, dammit! He must have forgotten who I was.

He was mad about Tony for no reason. Tony was a nonfactor. Tony was a popular BCAA football player who gave me attention and I let myself get wrapped up in it. But *he* wasn't who I wanted.

Hours had gone by, but I felt like I'd just signed on to my social media. I was on pictures and posts from months ago. I went so far down the rabbit hole, I found myself on her page. Nina aka 'Black Barbie'. *Did he give her that damn name?* She wasn't even cute, at least not compared to me.

Rashad used to go ape shit over my freckles, but his new chick was so damn basic. Her body was beautiful, though. She didn't have any designer labels in her pictures, like the ones I wore. *What did he see in her? Look at her slender frame.* She was slim with curves and had a more womanly body than me. *Maybe that's why Rashad liked her.*

I was five feet and petite. If I didn't wear alluring clothes and keep my hair done, I could be mistaken for a middle schooler. *I should get my breasts and butt done. A fat ass would keep his attention.* I sounded crazy. I'd never considered cosmetic surgery before.

The sun was up when I started stalking their social media accounts, but now, the sky was devoid of its usually vibrant California hues. I zoomed in on the smoothie picture Rashad had posted and saw a sign for *Utopian Villas*—the name of her beachfront home location—in the background. I recognized the area, and I was on my way.

Nina's skin was like Nutella, and she put me in the mind of a pampered princess. There was a picture on her profile page of her and her parents and I wanted to vomit when I saw it. They looked so... happy. *Fuck this!* Why did she get a doting father while I got stuck with Lucifer himself? I hated that man and the thought of him sent a chill up my spine. *I'm acting crazy, just like him. I'm just like him. That's why I hate him so much.* There wasn't time to disagree with myself because my car sputtered the moment I made it on Nina's street. My adrenaline pumped, probably because it was after midnight, and I'd finished two energy drinks already. I would not be ignored. He couldn't just move on. *She's no better than me. Is she?* No. She's not, dammit. *She's living her best life with my ex and I'm having an argument with myself.*

My raven black Mazda needed oil. The check oil light had been on for over a week, but I wouldn't be deterred, rational thought be damned. Nina's place was almost an hour from my off-campus apartment. I was determined to get there, despite my potential car troubles. I wasn't going to hurt her, just shake her up a bit. I would teach Nina what could happen if you fucked with a bitch like me. She'd probably never been hit in her life. It was not fair.

I prayed my vehicle would at least run until I was close enough to get to her place without a long walk. I needed to be there now. I decided not to let it die on me. Instead, I pulled it off to the side of the street, a few feet behind a neighbor's car. I yanked the hood from my hoodie over my head and slipped from my car. I was stealthy when I closed the door and positive Nina lived about five or six houses down.

As I continued the rest of the way on foot, my mind reeled. Nina was carefree. I wondered what it would feel like to be comfortable in my skin. What was it like to smile in pictures the way she did? I wondered if maybe I was jealous. Either way, this bitch needed to fall back.

Nina backed out of her driveway and left her house as I approached. It was almost one a.m. *Was she on her way to see him now?* My jaw clenched as I took in the colorful scarf that adorned her hair. She looked ethereal, like a brown goddess. A groan of irritation escaped my throat. When did the bohemian replace the vixen as the object of Rashad's affection? My heartbeat accelerated and sounded like an up-tempo snare drum. I felt my palms perspire; they were balled into fists and clasped tightly.

I bounced and shifted the weight between my feet as if I'd trained for a professional fight. She had to return home, eventually. I had time today. *Who does Nina think she is?* I would make *sure* she didn't stay a cheerful wench for long.

One

〜

NATE

I COULDN'T COMPREHEND how D had found her after all this time. He'd said he wouldn't rest until he did, and I respected him for it. I believed *he* believed he'd find her, but I never actually thought it could be done. D—my childhood next-door neighbor—had been in love with my sister from the first time he crashed his bike to stare at her. I got a kick out of his infatuation with her and didn't mind it. I figured D was an extra set of eyes to look out for Talley. In the end, none of us were able to keep her safe.

I'd made peace with the fact that my baby sister, NaTalley Brown, was dead—murdered and dumped somewhere like she was a piece of trash. The whole experience robbed me of my childhood. I used school to cope and avoid processing the trauma of being the sibling of a missing child. As an alternative to losing my young mind, I focused my energy and graduated high school at sixteen. I finished my undergraduate degree early, at eighteen, because I took a ton of general education college courses in high school. I'd graduated law school and passed the bar a few months before I could legally drink at a bar. I was officially Nathaniel Brown Esq. or Nathaniel Brown, PLLC; at least that was what the door to my office said.

When D called me, I thought he'd lost his mind. I half-listened to him and simultaneously tried to think of which psychiatrist I could call on his behalf. It had been ten years since she went missing. *Ten years*. I'd done all the tortuous research on how each day the child was missing, the chance of finding them decreased while the probability of finding them alive reduced exponentially. He'd insisted this wasn't a girl he thought was Talley or looked a lot like her; it was, in fact, her.

D nagged me until I agreed to contact a street therapist/preacher named Pastor Trey to arrive at my house to facilitate Talley's reunion. It was the home I grew up in. My parents passed it to me because the memories of Talley haunted my mom too much to live there any longer. I, however, loved it. Our home was an ever-present reminder of why I hustled the way I did. It might also be the reason my hair had gray patches—my unprocessed grief or practicing law with people twice my age and half my life experience.

When Talley was taken from us, I detached from the sadness her disappearance left in her place. I ignored it completely, but her arrival to my home knocked the wind out of me. She'd grown up and appeared to be unscathed. She couldn't remember me. I didn't know how to process all of it, but I was beyond grateful she was OK. My mom and dad handled it the best they could, and in the end, D was right about the need for Pastor Trey. He helped us navigate a situation we'd never fathomed. D remained like more of a brother to me through the years after my sister's disappearance, but when he reunited Talley with us, I knew I would forever be indebted to him.

I saw D each time he was home to visit his parents, and more often, since Talley's return. Yet, he continually proposed that I come out to ENEP's campus to visit him there. He wanted me to relocate, and I wasn't opposed to the idea. I'd officially put a visit to D's school at the top of my to-do list.

The past instability of my upbringing was an asset to my career. Other people attended social events and took vacations; I worked. I enjoyed the challenge of the law. More recently, I felt I'd taken on more than I could sustain. I had a feeling it was related to the loss of motivation now that my urge to escape was gone. I didn't have the fact that I hadn't kept my baby sister safe over my head anymore. *What the hell was I going to do about work now?*

. . .

I'D RECENTLY FINISHED my first trial and was exhausted, despite the amount of sleep I'd caught up on in the past week. The case lasted a whopping three years. I'd successfully assisted in the defense of my client and won them double what they were owed for their wrongful termination case. What the public didn't understand about law was I never *really* won. People called me with real-life problems I couldn't solve. The best I could do was deliver an outcome they could live with. My client was a thirty-five-year-old man who lost his job after he submitted a complaint to HR about repeated micro and macroaggressions he experienced at his corporate job.

We'd won the case and he'd been awarded more money than he thought he'd get. Nevertheless, for three years, he was without a steady job. He worked in a specialized field and was essentially blackballed. The other side, the legal team who represented his company, filed paperwork religiously to delay the inevitable trial. His wife had to work more hours outside of their home and, as a result, their relationship suffered. He'd been ostracized from work colleagues who were part of his friend circle; he'd worked with them since college. His two small children— one in elementary and one in middle school—got into fights because the other kids bullied them. Ultimately, years of gaslighting resulted in a lump sum of money that would keep two to three future generations of their family comfortable.

When all was said and done, I think what my client wanted most was his job. The one thing he enjoyed and was good at was taken from him, and I was incapable of giving it back. It was a theme for me. I wanted and tried to help but fell short.

I was supposed to protect my baby sister, but I'd let my parents down. As her older brother, I was expected to watch out for her. It was my job and I failed. Ironically, I'd landed in a field with the same dysfunctional dynamic. I spent a good majority of my young life with the law and was determined to spend my career, practicing in the courtroom. Maybe it was time for a change.

Despite the end of the trial, I still needed to show up to the office to access a few files and respond to some emails. I was ready to request some much-needed time off. After catching up with my little sister and the success of my first case, I needed some R&R. My office was humble, to say the least. Each time I entered the barely up-to-code building, I felt like an idiot. The person I rented the space from made triple what I did, and I couldn't be sure he had one degree in comparison to my professional ones. I was in the wrong damn field.

"There's some important people in your office," Gladys said unenthusiastically. "One of them looks like she's a model. Maybe an actress. She's too short to be a model."

Before I had time to ask more questions, Gladys turned her back to me and opened the door to the breakroom. I rolled my eyes and wiped the sleep from my face. I walked the few steps down the vacant hallway, toward my office, and cursed under my breath. Gladys was one of those employees who was older and did whatever she wanted. She was beyond retirement age, but more importantly, the wife of the owner of our small law practice. There was no use in asking her to screen my calls or visitors.

My phone buzzed in the pocket of my beige satchel. It was time for me to upgrade the bag, which was a present from my parents when I found out I'd been accepted into law school. It held sentimental value, but the material had seen better days.

I pulled out my smartphone and saw a message from D.

D: *it's a blessing from the ancestors big bro.*

Along with his text and a pair of brown praying hands, there was a hyperlink. The link redirected me to ENEP's website and an open position for a visiting law professor. I smiled to myself at his persistence and wondered what D had against blessings from Black Jesus.

I imagined what a relocation from Ohio to California might entail. I pictured beautiful, topless women and promptly scolded myself for my ignorance at what life at ENEP would be. I went through the motions as I entered my office. I'd momentarily forgotten about the warning of my visitors. I saw this girl's smooth skin and pouty lips immediately. She was physically tiny, but her energy was Godzilla sized. She wore the typical famous female entertainer attire—giant sunglasses, oversized hooded sweatshirt, sweatpants, and a handbag that probably cost a year of my salary. It was

Zanaé, the mega famous, sexy-as-shit pop star, and she was seated in my chair.

I tried to blink myself awake and concentrate, but her floral perfume put me into a metaphorical trance. I noticed a behemoth-sized man with a mean mug on his face. *He must be her bodyguard.* He stood a few yards away from a much smaller man with skin as velvety as Zanaé's. *Publicist or agent.*

"Hello," I said. I tried not to stare at her. I'd gone my whole life, successful in my dealings with women. They served an essential purpose, but they were also an obvious distraction. I'd seen lots of men I admired, who were in their prime, announce they would scale back at work for some chick—be it their wife or mistress.

I'd vowed to never make those mistakes because there was shit that needed to be done. I got my physical needs met, but what was the preoccupation? Why was there a sudden inability to focus on other shit after a man slept with an attractive woman? My answer sat directly in front of me. I would put in my notice today for a hug from her. She looked cozy as hell in my chair.

"Hello," I said again, like an idiot.

"You already said that," the cocoa butter-skinned guy said. He heaved a sigh, as if he did not have time for my drooling. "Look, we're here for a Nathaniel Brown. Is he your boss or something? Can you please get him? It's urgent!" His posture made it clear he needed this meeting done an hour ago.

"Uh."

He rolled his eyes at me, exasperated. "She's out of your league and unavailable," he muttered under his breath. *Well, damn, not that I thought I had a chance.*

"It's you." We all turned our gaze back to the "elephant" in the room. Zanaé was the sexiest elephant I'd ever had the pleasure of laying my eyes on. And her voice... I'd never heard anything so provocative, and all she'd said was, *"It's you."* I closed my eyes briefly and hoped nobody noticed.

"It's who?" the publicist squealed.

"He's Nathaniel Brown. I can tell. He's confident but not overly so," she said to them, then turned her gaze back toward me. I gulped. I hadn't moved from beside the door since I recognized her. "You're calm, though you're having a hard time keeping your cool with me. You're maintaining your composure out of personal respect for me—not because your job requires decorum—because your body language is saying fuck this job." She giggled and the sound sent sensations down my entire body.

"You're young as fuck, but you work a lot. You might work too much, but that's the reason you're so good. You need a vacation, some sleep, and maybe the company of a lady friend," she finished with a smirk.

Did she practice Hoodoo or something? Was she on D's ancestral vibes, or was my life simply transparent? She'd just read me like an online gossip headline.

As if by some evil coincidence, Yazmin, my assistant, barged into my office. The bodyguard shifted his attention quickly and lethally.

"Ohhhh, you're in a little meeting," Yazmin said, clearly unable or unwilling to read the room. "I thought I'd bring you breakfast. You never eat, and you left in such a hurry this morning," she kept on.

Sweat beaded on my brow and my Bloomingdale's stretch fit shirt dampened beneath my tailored suit jacket. Not only was this whole scene highly unprofessional, but I also did not want Zanaé to think I was romantically connected to an employee. *I must be crazy. This is* the *Zanaé. She is not interested in my Midwest raised, unfamous self.* I blew out a breath. *Fuck you. And shut up so I can try to manage the shit show about to happen if I don't get Yazmin out of my office.*

"I guess I was wrong about the company of a lady part," Zanaé amended.

"Uh, no," was all I could manage. Zanaé's eyes bore into me. I felt like she could see right through me, though her sunglasses remained on her beautiful face. Once again, she'd read me like a menu at a restaurant she was disinterested in and prepared to leave. But she was wrong about my involvement with Yazmin.

Chuckles then sighs from the publicist let me know my time was limited with them. They were clearly here for legal counsel, and I needed to address whatever concerns or questions they had.

I took a steadied breath and said, "This is my personal assistant.

She's been with me a few months now and is still learning the importance of either being a shadow or waiting until my meetings are over before interjecting."

"Personal assistant?" the publicist asked. His tone mirrored the suspicion of a woman I dated in the past who believed nothing I told her. He said it as though he didn't buy my shit and believed there was more to my relationship with Yazmin than met the eye.

Yazmin was stunning. She had unrealistic beauty and most people found her aesthetic annoying and unnerving. She graduated from ENEP in California where D went to school, but moved back to Ohio to be close to her parents. Even I wondered what it must be like to go through life with her looks; she could be a doppelgänger for Nicole Ari Parker, Boris Kodjoe's wife.

Her favorite story to tell was when Boris Kodjoe walked up to her and her Beta Delta Delta sorority sisters during a brunch. They were seated outside when he made his way past their table. He halted near her chair, stunned and speechless. He eventually found his words and said, "You look like my wife." She giggled and her sorority sisters screamed. Apparently, he physically shook his head back and forth, winked at her, and continued on with his day. He also paid for everyone's meal.

Yazmin was only twenty-five, but insanely efficient. We were technically the same age but light-years of difference in terms of life experience. The loss—or perceived loss—of a sibling aged me horribly. I was about ninety percent certain she wasn't interested in me, she just had an immense amount of sexual energy. Yazmin loved men and she didn't hide it. She enjoyed her girl time, but preferred male friends and male bosses.

"When you're fine like this, there's no way to be a shadow. Kim K was a personal assistant; look at her now. Not that I want any parts of her lifestyle. Anyways, you know my daddy was a lawyer, Nate, so I get it. You're busy. But he also needed help taking care of regular human things, like eating. I apologize to the room for interrupting and calling this a 'little' meeting. Certainly, a meeting with Zanaé isn't little." She whispered when she said 'Zanaé,' as if someone else would overhear the conversation.

Zanaé's bodyguard laughed, and Yazmin shot him a smile I swear made him blush. "Like I was saying, I'm leaving now, but at least drink the protein smoothie. The last thing you want is to faint... again," she said as she sashayed out of my office.

"Well, damn," the publicist said. "I like her!"

"Thank you. And as much as I'm enjoying your company, I suppose you're not here for small talk. Why was my name mentioned to you all? Are you in need of legal consultation?" I asked as I regained my composure.

The air in the room shifted, and the energy was suddenly tense.

Two

VERONICA

MY MEETING with Everest Northern Engineering Program's (ENEP) Student Rights and Conduct Committee was scheduled for eight-thirty a.m. on the Monday morning following my arrest for posting the video of Nina and my ex, Rashad. Campus police released me after a few hours because no one officially pressed charges. I was given the details for my appointment with ENEP employee investigators on my way out. The arresting officer made it clear I was not to interact with Rashad or Nina, and I could not attend class, nor could I return to campus until after the meeting.

I was convinced they selected the early time to punish me. There were occasions where I was awake at this hour, but I certainly wasn't dressed and outside of my apartment. I walked into the sterile building at eight twenty-seven a.m. Its layout put me in the mind of a prison as opposed to a college.

I tried a semi-professional look but opted to keep my matte black aviators on to hide my puffy eyes. I'd been crying non-stop since I was arrested. Until then, I'd never had any fallout for my bad bitch antics. An arrest shook the shit out of me.

I wore white dress pants and a white, fitted blazer I'd had tailored to fit my small frame. Underneath the blazer, I wore a cream camisole. My jet-black hair remained straight, despite my refusal to maintain it. I kept my long tresses wrapped and underneath a scarf on the car ride over, then combed it down quickly once I settled in the parking lot.

I navigated to the room indicated on the paper the officers gave me and checked my Tambour slim-fit Louis Vuitton watch. The white band and rose gold face revealed the time to be eight twenty-nine a.m. I tried to increase my pace, but my stilettos were already killing me.

"Oh, don't go in there like that."

I turned to see an annoyingly tempting chocolate kid who peered down at me. Ugh, the Lord knew a deep bronze man was my weakness. I guessed he was a student since he wore an all-black ENEP hoodie, but his beard had patches of gray, so I couldn't be sure. He had a salt and pepper colored fade with waves that would make any girl seasick.

I could appreciate the "print" in his black sweatpants. I let my eyes bulge since I wore my sunglasses and knew my eyes wouldn't betray my arousal. He had his lip tucked beneath the top row of his pearly white teeth as he scrutinized my figure.

Something about the small space between his top teeth made the center of my thighs melt. I took a deep breath to focus my attention, but immediately regretted it. He smelled of cedar, citrus, and shea butter. *Good Lordt!*

I didn't have time for this. *What did he say?*

"What?" I propped my hand on my hip.

"You don't want to go in there in those clothes. At least take your glasses off," this sexy ass stranger insisted in a deep, gruff voice. I just knew he could fuck from the sound of his voice alone.

"What's it to you? And I'm not interested, if that's what you're getting at."

"Damn, OK." He scratched the back of his head, and when he lifted his long arm, I saw his muscle flex. The motion made my pulse quicken. *Bitch, you need to get laid. You're so damn embarrassing.* "Uh, you're obviously attractive, but whatever it is you're seeing them about, it's not going to go in your favor if you show up looking like an entitled celebrity."

Who the hell did he think he was? And who gave him the right to question me? I didn't have time for this. It was eight-thirty a.m., and I would be late if I didn't end this conversation now.

He raised his hands in surrender, and I saw his arms strain through his black hoodie. *Did they make fitted hoodies, or was this dude buff as hell? He would probably toss me around easily with a set of arms like those.* "Don't say you weren't warned. My name is Nathaniel Brown, but you can call me Nate." He winked as he introduced himself to me like I gave a damn.

"Chantel," I huffed before I realized what I'd said.

"Chantel? I like it a lot."

"I mean, Veronica." I had no idea why this man had me frazzled. I guess I didn't want him to associate me with Bad Bitch V.

"I see. You give out fake names when you're not interested." Nate's eyes danced with delight and all I could do was try not to fidget.

"It's my first name. I usually don't offer it to strangers. Look, I have to go."

"I'm sure I'll be seeing you around, pretty lady."

He was sexy as hell, but like I said, I wasn't interested. I rolled my eyes and grabbed the cold door handle to the staff office door marked 2111. I added a sway to my hips because I'd bet my favorite Christian Louboutins, Nate's eyes escorted me into the room.

Once inside, I noted three employees seated behind a long desk. They laughed at something and held a relaxed demeanor until their eyes collided with me. The only female employee let her gaze travel from my bone straight hair to my Louis Vuitton timepiece. She scowled as her eyes slid in the direction of the purple, suede Jimmy Choos I wore on my feet to match my neon green Beta Delta Delta Greek letter lapel pin. Fine Ass Nate was right. I'd just fucked myself.

A caramel-complected man with a bald head and beautifully maintained beard—the older of the three—had kind eyes and gave me a quick, warm smile. The last employee of the Students Rights and Conduct Committee investigators cleared his throat as he tried to keep his eyes on anything but me.

"Sit down, Chantel," the woman said with agitation. I hated for anyone other than family to use my first name. "I'm Liz, this is Donald to my left, and Eric to my right. We'll oversee gathering information regarding your case."

"I'd prefer to be called Veronica, please," I amended.

"That's fine. I usually go by Don. Donald makes me feel like my mother is in the room," the older gentleman said in an easy tone. He was an ally, and I was relieved at least one of them was on my side. I wasn't sure if Liz could be won over, but there was still hope for Eric.

I removed my aviators and sat awkwardly in the chair across the room from them. There was no desk in front of me, so I berated myself to be still. *Don't fidget!* I attempted to sit confidently, but I was so nervous. I felt guilty. *Bitch, you are guilty!*

"Let's get started. For clarity, state your full name," Liz began.

"Chantel Veronica Waters. But I go by Veronica."

"Veronica, we're going to ask you a series of questions, and it's imperative you be honest with us. We are not in charge of what happens with the information we find. Final decisions will be up to the Dean of Students and the special assistant to ENEP's President, Nathaniel Brown.

"He is a visiting law professor, and more recently, he's become a consulting expert on cases like yours. He'll probably be around if you're needed in the dean's office," Don added.

"Dammit," I said under my breath.

"Is there a problem, Veronica?" Liz asked.

"No, ma'am. I saw him on the way in and mistook him for a student."

"No need for ma'ams around here. He is *not* a student; he's a professor who happened to be in sweats today. I suggest you focus on the matter at hand. Maybe if you prioritize school over boys, you wouldn't be in this situation."

"OK. Liz, be cool," Eric said as he passed them each a manilla folder.

They opened the folders, and I saw printed copies of my social media profile page and stills of the video I'd posted. It was a screen grab that had been blown up so the time and caption were easy to see.

"Is your social media handle 'that girl V B'?" Don asked, pronouncing the Greek letter symbols Beta Delta Delta as B triangle, triangle.

"Yes, sir. I mean, yes."

"Try not to be too nervous. I'm fine with sir or Don. We're just collecting your account of the events at this point. We are not here to judge you."

"OK. Yes. That's my social media handle."

"What does V B mean, exactly?" Eric quired, parroting the B triangle, triangle instead of their true annunciation.

"Those are her sorority Greek letters. She's wearing the pin on her expensive blazer now," Liz interjected with a loud sigh before I could respond to the question. She acted as if she didn't like me from the moment I walked in.

"Liz, are you sure you can remain impartial? You belong to their rival sorority. Weren't you the chapter president of Sigma Lambda Lambda when you were a student at ENEP?" Don questioned.

He was like a brown guardian angel. I'd done so much problematic shit, at times, it was hard to speak up for myself when I needed to. She was way out of line.

"You are correct. I did serve as the chapter president of Sigma Lambda Lambda, Omega Alpha chapter. I apologize, Veronica. I'll be sure to check our innocuous rivalry at the door. While we are in the confines of this room, I will not let my letters affect my ability to gather information and advocate for you if the incident calls for it."

"Thank you," I said, though I suddenly felt the urge to cry. The hell? *I don't cry, I get what I want.* Right now, though, I struggled to believe my own BS.

"At four thirty-five p.m. on Friday, October 13th, there is a post from your social media account of a night vision video. The video appears to feature two ENEP students. A seventeen-year-old, Nina Jordan, and a nineteen-year-old, Rashad Hill, engaging in sexual activity.

"The uploaded video is a thirty-second clip that plays on a loop with music added. Does this video look familiar?" Eric asked. He shifted uncomfortably at the mention of the video and the question he needed to ask.

"Yes."

"Did you post this video?" Don asked.

I sat quietly and hung my head for several minutes. What the hell was I supposed to do here? I couldn't bring myself to lie. Tears dripped down my face and I brushed them away quickly before I ended up with raccoon eyes from smeared makeup. I *never* cried—I got even. But look where that got me.

"I did something awful here, and I honestly don't know if I'd be crying if I didn't get caught. Until I got arrested, I didn't see a damn thing wrong with what I did. I was... I mean, I am in a really dark place. Rashad Hill is my ex. I don't deserve him, but when I learned he'd moved on with Nina, something in me snapped. I think I'm losing my mind or something.

"I recorded the video because I went there to... I don't know... confront her. Then I saw them on her balcony. I only turned my phone on so I could see them closer. I was more than mad; I was enraged. I had no idea they would start having sex." I took a deep breath because I started hyperventilating between words. I was a bitch, but I wasn't a monster like people were making it seem.

"When they started doing it, I wasn't pissed anymore. I was mortified. I don't even know why I hit record. I felt like he liked her more. It looked like he enjoyed her more than he did when he was with me." *Bitch, you sound like a nutcase.* I exhaled audibly in both frustration and sadness. "No person should ever see an ex have sex—especially if you aren't over them. It would make anyone crazy.

"I smashed my phone against the dashboard of my car out of anger after I recorded, so I honestly had no intention of doing anything with the footage. But once I got home, I couldn't let it go. I retrieved the video from my iCloud. Curiosity got the best of me, and even though I knew it was cruel and unusual punishment for myself, I rewatched it.

"Anyway, I added the music from my laptop because you could hear me crying and cursing loudly in the background. I hardly ever cry. I felt so pathetic, and I just wanted to feel better. So, I posted what I saw with that horrible caption." *Bitch, have you ever heard of self-incrimination? I gotta do everything around here. You gone fuck around and get us locked up. Bad bitch, my ass.* My own voice taunted me. Maybe I was losing it.

"I only wanted to break them up," I went on. Because why not at this point? "I figured if she thought he posted it, they'd break up. I never considered it would humiliate her in the process. I didn't know it was her first time, and I certainly didn't know she was under eighteen."

They all looked at me with their mouths open. I was sure I'd be kicked out of school. I'd said too damn much. But it would have killed me to lie just to keep up my bad bitch persona; it had to come out.

"I'm not a monster, even though what I did was disgusting. I think maybe I need help." *Bitch, is you crazy?* I dropped my head into my hands and sobbed. This must be what rock bottom felt like. After a few moments, there was a hand on my shoulder, and when I looked up, it was Liz. She stood beside me with a handful of Kleenex.

"It takes a lot of strength to admit what you did. I'm proud of you," she said.

Her empathetic words didn't help. *Pity from a Sigma Lambda Lambda? You are pathetic!* I cried harder. She leaned down and hugged me and let me cry all the tears I'd been holding since I was little.

"Thank you, Liz," I cried. "Thank you!"

"Now, Veronica, while we appreciate your honesty, ENEP reserves the right to withdraw you as a student. The consequences for your social misconduct could be steep, and I advise you to prepare yourself," Don added gently yet firmly.

"We are all rooting for you, but as we asked Liz to do, we must remain as impartial as possible, especially since your actions had a negative impact on the safety of another student who was a minor at the time of the incident," was Eric's contribution.

The fact that they were able to hold me accountable without shame made it easier for me to hold my head up and back straight. I was ready for whatever the dean would decide.

"I understand."

MY HEAD WAS BURIED under my favorite couch blanket, despite it being well into the afternoon when Jess, the Beta Delta Delta chapter president, texted me. I'd barely rested the past few nights. I slept only from exhaustion when my eyes became too tired for whatever movie or episode was on in the background. Today, I was on the couch after I decided I was too tired to put on clothes or leave my apartment.

My cellphone was by my face when the alert's vibration shook me from my second sleep.

B chpt pres: *V, have you seen the verdict? You're suspended from all campus organizations, including Beta activities, for the rest of the semester. Pick up your phone.*

I checked the home screen of my smart phone again and, sure enough, I had three missed calls from her.

Me: *what???*

B chpt pres: *Get your ass up and check your email! I got one from the dean's office saying you are not to participate in any Beta activities or hold any offices. Sad eyes emoji. I'm going to have to appoint someone else to organize our ice breaker/party details. I'm sorry girl. Call me when you get up and let me know you're OK.*

Dammit! I pulled myself up on the couch. I'd met with the Student Rights and Conduct Committee on Monday and the dean had a decision for me already? It was only Wednesday. I clicked on my phone's mail app and located an email from the Office of the Dean.

Chantel Veronica Waters,

It is the decision of Everest Northern Engineering Program to charge the following sanctions for the social media misconduct/harassment involving two other ENEP students. At this time, Nina Jordan is refusing to take legal action and does not seek action at the collegiate level, however, since the incident involves ENEP students, we've decided that you will/(are):

- *Resign from any offices held with any campus organizations*
- *Suspended from participation in any campus organization for the remainder of the academic semester*
- *Lose privileges to dine in campus dining halls for the remainder of the academic semester*
- *Lose privileges to attend any campus games, events, or ENEP social related activities for the remainder of the academic semester*

- *NOT contact either Nina Jordan or Rashad Hill via any social platform for the remainder of your time at ENEP*

THE FOLLOWING ARE **REQUIRED** *ACTIONS (If ENEP finds you non-compliant of the listed above or below, you will be suspended or face expulsion)*

- ***Mandatory Weekly Counseling Sessions*** *for the remainder of your time here at ENEP to begin immediately*
- ***Mandatory Weekly Community Service*** *for the remainder of your time here at ENEP to begin immediately*
- *You are to submit forms weekly to the dean's office to show signed proof of attendance at counseling and community service*

SEND *an email acknowledging that you received this message within twenty-four hours and Contact Dean Williams or Nathaniel Brown with any questions.*

DOUBLE DAMN!

Three

NATE

IT HAD BEEN over a month since Zanaé and her team visited my Cincinnati office. Before they could tell me how I could help, her publicist received a call that demanded they drop everything. Zanaé shook my hand before they left, and I swear I almost screamed. I didn't, though. Her publicist swiftly had me sign an NDA. With an excess of adrenaline, I'd applied to the job from D's message and figured I probably wouldn't hear back.

I did hear back, and things moved at lightning speed. The president was so impressed with my credentials, he requested an online interview to expedite the hiring process. Within two weeks, I'd accepted a visiting professor position with ENEP. The temporary move would give me time to sort out what type of law I wanted to practice. During law school, I'd learned about the numerous avenues I could take with my career, but I'd been sure I only wanted to practice law in court. I hoped this new position as a visiting professor would give me insight to what else I might enjoy.

I clicked with the president right away. He was a man of integrity who didn't take himself too seriously. He had the level of confidence in his profession—despite those who sought to undermine him—I aspired to. Besides the intro to law class I'd teach, I'd also consult on social misconduct cases. President Samuel Reed saw to it that all I needed to do was board my plane and select one of the many luxury accommodations he suggested. Everything else associated with my temporary relocation would be handled.

I chose Utopian Villas because it reminded me of the movies I watched about life in California when I was younger. I had several boxes unpacked in each room, but I was in no hurry to tend to them. I stood at the opened patio door of my two-bedroom villa and analyzed why I'd never moved out of Ohio or taken a legitimate vacation.

Talley appeared in my mind's eye. She was the reason I'd stuck around. I lived in our old home because she felt close there. And thanks to D, my family discovered she had been close. She'd been a few hours away from us the entire time. The feeling brought a sense of comfort to me, but haunted my parents.

Now that we'd been reunited with her, I no longer felt tethered to Ohio. I missed Talley, but my goal would be to get her to visit me here. I was sure D would love to see her again. I decided as soon as I was settled, I'd do what I could to make a visit with Talley at ENEP happen.

My stomach rumbled, and though I was a mostly pleasant human being, I became a different person when I was hungry. I didn't need to worry about how I'd be fed for most of my life because I lived at home for most of my college career. Law school was a whole different world. No one cared how young I was and that I had no clue how to feed myself, but I learned quickly.

I taught myself out of necessity and ended up with a brand-new superpower. I cooked my way through law school because I was broke. I didn't have a wealthy family or a lineage of lawyers like my classmates, so while they ordered food for late-night study sessions, I cooked.

The first few months were terrible. I undercooked and overcooked everything I tried. But after a few thousand YouTube videos and conversations with older women in the local markets, I adjusted. My food went from edible, to pleasant, to a bona fide side hustle. I became the student other students paid to cook what they called 'a home-cooked meal'. I invested an extra hour or so to make plenty of food for my cohort and ended up with an excess of money to cover my additional expenses, along with enough to take a lady friend out from time to time.

Now, however, with a new job and the major transition of a state-to-state move, the last thing I wanted to do was go to the grocery store and cook. I dressed and decided to drive to the location of my new job.

The drive was peaceful, though I still hadn't fully adjusted to California drivers. The pace and speed of traffic was fine; it was the lack of concern for another person's safety that drove me nuts.

I found my way back to campus and decided ENEP's dining would do. The students on ENEP's campus were all esthetically pleasing. They made the people in Ohio look downright unfortunate in comparison. I shook my head and chuckled to myself. I felt shallow as hell for the thought, but I'd be a damn lie if I didn't acknowledge how stunning the women were. The instructors weren't bad, either. *I need to get laid before I do something dumb like end up in a relationship I can't sustain.*

The amount of lush green present on campus blew my mind. Everything in Cincinnati was gray this time of year. I walked away from employee parking with pep in my step. I liked it here. I arrived at the steps of the student union and continued to take in my new surroundings.

"Hey." I turned my body to see whose sultry voice made my dick jump. *It hadn't been that long since I got some, had it?* I went through a mental rolodex to remember. Yeesh, almost three months. I dropped my gaze to her petite frame to meet her eyes.

"Chantel? I mean, Veronica," I amended. I didn't want to call her by her first name like a creep when she said she hadn't meant to give it to me. I just liked it so much. It seemed to suit her better, in my opinion. She had a NY ball cap on her head. If it was her attempt to conceal her looks, she was crazy as hell. I found her as attractive in her sweats as I did when I saw her fully dressed up.

I'd spoken with her briefly in the Students' Rights building a couple weeks ago and I had to mentally tell myself not to reach out and touch her then. She'd stood there, frustrated with my advice, and all I could visualize were lewd scenes of her face smashed into the mattress on my bed. I couldn't put my finger on what it was about Veronica I was captivated by. I was a man who played by the rules. I spent my young life in a career where procedures, bylaws, and decrees were my bread and butter, yet something about this woman intrigued me.

I knew she must have been in some sort of trouble if she was in that building for an eight-thirty a.m. meeting. They picked those times to punish the students, something I never agreed with as a tactic. I felt like a straightforward approach was the most respectful and reasonable method.

Veronica was pissed when I told her not to go inside, dressed in her stilettos, designer bag, and designer shades, and it somehow made her more attractive to me. She was the first woman I'd ever encountered who didn't break their neck to take my advice and follow my lead. I had a few ideas on how I could get her to comply. *Shit, I must be out of my mind.*

It wouldn't technically break any rules if I became involved with her, but it would be frowned upon because of the power dynamic. I'd just turned twenty-five and she couldn't be any more than twenty. She hadn't done anything but say 'hey' and stand there, yet her presence overwhelmed my senses. Veronica smelled of mint and something else I couldn't identify; together, the sweet mint reminded me of dessert. I fucking loved dessert.

"Hello. Nathaniel Brown." She snapped her fingers playfully in my face. I'd zoned out and stood there, deep in my thoughts. I refocused my attention on her small face. With her head craned up at me from one of the lower steps, the sun hit her at the perfect angle. She had freckles, and I felt an urge to trace them with my finger. She wasn't close enough for me, so I descended a few steps and closed the space between us as inconspicuously as I could.

"Yeah, um, my bad." I acted like I'd never spoken to an attractive woman. I may have spent my time in the Midwest, but I'd kept the contacts of a few bad bitches. Nevertheless, this one felt risky, and the risk element had me tempted.

"You want to come inside the union? I'm starving, and I'd like to focus when I speak with you," I admitted. I put myself out there and held my breath for her likely rejection. She probably had a boyfriend. Veronica was probably used to a different caliber of man. I did alright when it came to money, but I didn't have California or entertainer lifestyle funds by any means.

"I'm sorry, I can't. But I wanted to thank you for trying to save me a few weeks back. They were not pleased with the way I was dressed. You tried to warn me."

"Yeah, not a problem. Did everything go OK? I wasn't given your case. I mean, I'm attached to it by name only. So far, they haven't asked me to consult on it. I've given feedback on several, but your name hasn't been mentioned. I guess stealing cookies from a rival sorority doesn't require my expertise." She tensed at my joke, and I wanted to take it back. Maybe she had done something unspeakable.

"I... Everything went OK. I guess you could say. I better go. I just wanted to thank you for the heads up about the committee."

I metaphorically kicked myself for shoving my size thirteens in my mouth and watched as she slinked away from me. She wore baggy sweatpants, yet her ass still jiggled enough to keep my attention. How someone could be so little with such presence was a mystery to me.

I wasn't sure if she cut our conversation short because I'd offended her or if she had a man, but she rejected my offer when I asked her to come inside with me while I ate. I also wondered if my joke about the sorority bothered her. The pull toward Veronica had me puzzled as hell, and my empty stomach didn't help the situation. Food would make my brain settle and hopefully forget about Bad Girl Chantel Veronica.

THE CAMPUS FOOD wasn't bad. It was overpriced as hell, but not bad. On the days I wasn't up for cooking or had to stay late at work, I'd eat there again. I still hadn't unpacked my things, so I bought a shirt, a pair of shorts, and socks from the bookstore to work out on campus. All the gear had ENEP plastered across the front and down the leg, but I didn't mind since it would get sweaty, anyway.

I wanted to see what the recreation center offered, and if I'd make the drive from my new home to work out or if I'd join a gym. I worked out religiously. When I didn't, I wasn't myself. I'd try any kind of workout once. It didn't have to be basketball or weightlifting, even though those were my favorite go-to workouts on a stressful day. I'd done distance runs, CrossFit, and mixed martial arts. Any activity that got me into my body and out of the stress in my head would do.

I brought my heavy bag from Ohio to practice kickboxing when I needed an immediate stress reliever. Now that I was on the West Coast, I hoped to maybe climb a mountain if I could work up the nerve. Outdoor runs would be much more enjoyable here than in the cold weather from home.

ENEP's campus was picturesque. It was as impressive as the women. I took in my surroundings as I wandered from the bookstore to the employee parking where my shoes were in the trunk of my Lincoln. While the people and the internal features of the campus were pristine, the exterior of the buildings were historic. My mind wandered back to Veronica on my walk. Curiosity caused me to post up against my car and find the details of her case.

I navigated to student files from the app on my phone and located her case. *Chantel Veronica Waters harassment case.* The hell? I clicked the link and the phone nearly slipped from my hands as perspiration beaded in my palms. I didn't want to learn anything I couldn't overlook, yet the need to know outweighed my ability to use reason. I'd already clicked the file, and there was no way I wouldn't read it now.

Student Chantel Veronica Waters admits to recording fellow students, Rashad Hill and Nina Jordan, during sexual activity at Nina's home without their permission.

My eyes widened as I took in the details of her case.

She also admits to uploading the video to social media...

...she was unaware Nina Jordan was underage at the time of the incident and adds she later learned it was Jordan's first sexual experience. Waters expresses remorse to the Student Rights and Conduct Committee and admits she needs help.

I skimmed the case quickly.

She confesses she wanted to break them up, and thought if Jordan assumed the video was uploaded by Hill, an ex of Waters, she'd get what she wanted. Waters adds, she never considered how embarrassing sharing the video would be for Jordan and insists she didn't know it was her first sexual experience.

I was as shocked by the details as I was by her honesty around her behavior.

The Student Rights Committee, Donald Jones, Elizabeth White, and

Eric Smith, all recommend strong boundaries for Chantel Veronica Waters in the way of weekly community service and counseling. Each of the committee strongly disagrees with expulsion, especially since student Nina Jordan refuses to press charges.

As of today's date, Waters has complied with the expectations.

Shit!

I closed the app and released the breath I'd held the entire time I read her electronic file. No wonder she didn't think my joke was funny. It was a lot to wrap my head around, yet I surprisingly didn't have an ounce of judgment toward her. What I felt most as I read about Veronica's actions was empathy. She sounded so desperate, and the fact that she took accountability for what she'd done made me more fascinated with her. I needed my workout badly. It would help me sort all of this out in my head.

I popped the trunk of my car and grabbed a pair of sneakers. I locked up and journeyed back toward the center of campus. Everything in this city and at this school felt new and shiny. It wasn't always cloudy in Cincinnati, but the fall and winter were only picturesque during the first snow. After that, I could expect months of brown, slushy sleet because we needed to drive on the white pillowy blankets of snow—unlike the photos shared online. California had continual sunshine, and so far, I loved it.

Each building on ENEP's campus seemed to be miles from the next. The walk was so stimulating, I didn't mind. I looked at it as a warmup to my workout.

I felt like a teenager again when I stepped inside of ENEP's recreational center. Women of all shapes and sizes dressed in scantily clad workout gear filtered in and out. I had no idea where to put my eyes.

My classmates in law school complained we'd never fully experience typical college life. At the time, it sounded like a luxury for the privileged. I didn't know of anyone who looked like me who had the time or funds for a year to backpack around Europe. But as I stood in a sea of alluring women, I realized what they meant. I'd never had escapades like a typical student or like the ones D mentioned to me. I was too busy with and focused on my studies.

There was a massive row of ellipticals, stair steppers, bikes, and treadmills; they seemed to extend the length of the building. Cardio was where I preferred to start my workout. After my heart rate was up, I'd move to weights. The cardio machines faced huge racquetball courts with glass walls. Between the cardio area and the racquetball courts were oversized blue mats for stretching. I strolled over in their direction to get my body ready for the punishment I would inevitably endure.

"Hey, Professor." I turned to see Professor Walker. Vivian Walker was also a professor at ENEP. She wasn't quite as young as me, but I guessed her to be no more than thirty. Walker taught real estate law in the same building as my intro to law courses. She introduced herself to me the first day I stepped foot on campus. It was a struggle to be near her because I found her energy to be chaotic and overwhelming.

Professor Walker was dressed in one of those suggestive workout outfits the other female students wore. The flirtation dripped from her voice as she craned her neck up at me. She dropped to the blue mat below her and spread her legs to stretch. I choked on my spit because, the fuck? She hopped back up and the motion sent her titties in two different directions. Professor Walker patted me on the back to help with my cough, but what I needed was space and some consequence-free sex. I was positive I couldn't get it from her.

I held my hands up and mouthed, "I'm good." But I was far from good. Her pats morphed to rubs and my body responded. I cleared my throat again and created a safe distance between us. "Professor Walker. It's nice to see you."

She plopped back down on the blue mat. Walker resumed her stretches and slammed her head atop her knee. I looked around to ensure I wasn't the only one who saw this. Several male students smiled my way with nods of approval.

They probably would have given their last dime to be up close and personal with her, but I wasn't interested in a messy coworker situation. *But you wanna smash a student? Bad Girl Veronica wouldn't be messy?* I coughed two more times and finally thought about using the ENEP water bottle I held in my hands.

"Are you all settled?" she asked while she did the downward dog pose and lifted her leg. *Help me, Black Jesus!*

"I'm getting there. I'm here to sneak in a workout. Uh, yeah... I'll leave you to it." I hoped she'd let me be on my way because I could no longer think professional thoughts about Professor Walker.

"No problem! Our offices are near each other, so I'm sure I'll run into you soon." She smiled at me and bent over into a backbend. The gravity of her breasts about knocked her out and it made me relax. The shit was so funny. I kept my eyes downcast so I wouldn't see any more temptation and made my way to the basketball court. It seemed the safest area from distraction in the gym.

"Big bro!" D called out the moment I stepped into the large space.

"What up, D? The hell are you doing here? I know your basketball playing ass has your own personal gym. Ain't it like against the rules for you to play amongst us commoners?"

He walked over and gave me a bear hug. D was the only person I knew who was bigger than me. He'd always been a tall kid, but now that he was a collegiate level athlete, he was muscular as well. I was able to beat him one on one until he started at ENEP. Once he started training with other crazy talented students, I didn't stand a chance. I hoped his shorts and basketball sneakers meant maybe he'd run a few with me.

"I do what I want. This school don't own ya boy. Nah mean?"

"Is that right?"

"Yes, sir." D gave me his million-dollar smile and I couldn't help but laugh in response. He was like a brother to me, and for the past ten years, my only sibling. The only thing harder than the loss of my baby sister was seeing what it did to D. In many ways, I felt he was more negatively impacted by Talley's disappearance than I was. He became an exceptional basketball player, but the physical toll it took on him was apparent.

My trauma was hidden while D's was written all over him. I'd buried myself in law, and though I did have unexplainable gray hair, the effects of her kidnapping were well beneath the surface when it came to me.

"Let's play to ten so I can get a workout in. I can't concentrate for shit out there. Is this why you had me move to California? To be distracted by women twenty-four seven?"

"You talking about the chicks out there?" He laughed loudly. "If you're struggling with the students at ENEP, don't go off campus. You live in Utopian Villas? Don't leave your spot or go to the grocery store. Your old ass will fuck around and have a heart attack."

I couldn't help but join his laughter. I had no idea how anyone could get any work done when the women looked the way they did.

D's roommate and another student I didn't recognize made their way toward us. I wasn't familiar with Rashad. D seemed to vouch for his character, and if D fucked with him, he was good with me.

"Rashad, you remember my big bro, Nate?" D asked as he gripped him up in a ritualistic handshake.

"Talley's brother, right?" Rashad asked as he extended his hand toward me. "It's nice to finally meet you. D's ass is always going on and on about his brother, Nate, the attorney."

"Whatever, Rashad. Step aside. Nate, this is Rashad's homie, Kadeem from Chicago. He's here on leave from the military," D explained.

While Rashad was a fresh-faced kid who reminded me of a fourteen-year-old in a twenty-year-old's body, Kadeem had life experience tattooed across his face. I recognized the look because I had it. I couldn't imagine how his life was as a young black man in the military. I'd heard of soldiers who leveraged their time in the service to pay for school or build wealth and others who felt like the military fucked them over without so much as a thank you.

"Nice to meet you, man, and thank you for your service," I said as I shook his hand. "What branch are you in?"

"Air Force. And what kind of law do you practice? I could use a guy like you on my team," Kadeem said with a raspy chuckle.

"Civil rights law. But I'm taking a break to teach and see if I'll continue to practice trial law or switch it up."

"That's dope. Rashad's ass keeps some talented friends," Kadeem added in awe.

"Birds of a feather, my dude," Rashad said as he laced up his sneakers. We all appeared to be at least six feet with Rashad and Kadeem on the shorter side of the spectrum, but none of us was disillusioned about who had the skill on the court. D was here for fun, while we'd all be pushed to the edge, trying to keep up with him.

"Me and Nate against you and Kadeem," D said to Rashad.

"Fine by me. Chicago beats Cincinnati any day," Rashad said confidently.

Who was this kid?

THE GAME ENDED QUICKLY. D made the majority of the points. I scored a few, but Kadeem was strong as hell. When they did get the ball, Kadeem only scored on me once. I might not have been the best basketball player, but nobody but D could outwork me.

Surprisingly, D hadn't made Rashad look completely helpless. He'd kept up with D and all I could think was it had to be because they were together so much. He crossed D at one point and even I had to give him props for it. I got along with most people. I fit in with men and women of all types of backgrounds, but there was something about Rashad's shrill voice that bugged the shit out of me.

We made our way to the bleachers to cool off and hydrate. I did what I usually did when I didn't know people well: I listened and observed.

"What y'all been getting into?" D asked Kadeem and Rashad.

"I been showing my boy around. He about had a fit when he saw some of the Sigma Lambda Lambdas." Rashad laughed.

"They had on these tight little cut off sweaters and spandex pants. It looked like some shit I've seen on TV," Kadeem responded.

"They cute, but the sexiest sorority girls are the Beta Delta Deltas. Everybody knows that," D supplied.

"Speaking of Beta Delta Delta; we ran into Rashad's ex on the way in here," Kadeem boomed with a laugh.

"No shit? She still fine as hell?" D asked playfully, with his eyes on Rashad.

"Man, you can have her psycho ass. She's fine, but Veronica is crazy as bat shit," Rashad added as he lifted to stretch his body.

My pulse picked up. *Did he mean my Veronica? Shit. What was I on? She wasn't mine, but was it the same Veronica I knew and could admit I wanted to know better?*

"Veronica ain't crazy, man. She's young," D added a bit more seriously. He'd said it like he wasn't her same age, yet I knew his life experience made him more like a thirty-year-old man in terms of the way he moved through life.

"Man, fuck that bitch!" Rashad spat out.

Before I knew what happened, I stood. He was a few inches shorter than me, so he had to look up to meet my gaze.

"What's wrong with you? Your mama ain't teach you how to speak about women?"

"You don't know me to be asking about my moms." Rashad's chest swelled and I'd struck a chord with him at the mention of his mother. "And Veronica is a fucking bi—" he started.

I tussled him to the floor and I had no idea why. With my knee pressed in the center of his chest, I insisted in a deadly, calm tone, "Please don't refer to another woman as a bitch in front of me." The vein in my forehead pulsed, and I glared down at him like he had one more time.

"Aye, man." D and Kadeem rushed over. D pulled me off and Kadeem yanked Rashad's extra ass up from the floor. "You know he got a sister so he's sensitive about women," D said to Rashad. D seemed frazzled because I knew he wanted us to get along.

"You don't know what she did. Veronica put my girl out there and embarrassed her on the fucking internet. She ain't behaved shit like a woman, bro." He shrugged Kadeem off him angrily and stormed toward the exit.

The hell was I doing? I knew about the revenge porn Veronica posted, and the shit was deplorable. I was a man who believed in fairness. On one hand, Veronica did what the law and the school required her to do because of her behavior. So what else did they want from her? At the same time, the girl in the video was Rashad's new girlfriend, Nina, and she hadn't deserved to be put out there the way she had. I could see why he was pressed, but I still wanted to chase Rashad down and beat the shit out of him.

Kadeem gave D a nod and followed Rashad. D stood and faced the doors until they were no longer in view.

"Big bro, what the hell wa—" D started.

"Look, man, I'm under pressure with the move. Everyone and everything is different from back home." I told him a half-truth because I *was* stressed with the major life changes.

D gave me his half-smile. "If you say so." D examined me thoughtfully and I got the impression he could smell my interest in Veronica. I shifted my gaze to a few students who entered the gym. "About Rashad, he can be an ass, but he has a good heart. He's genuinely a good dude.

"And his girl Nina, she's fucking amazing! They recently found out she's pregnant, and he's on his macho, caveman protector shit even when she isn't in any actual danger." D chuckled to himself again. "You just have to meet her. I'd do the same for LaTonya."

"How is your thicker than a Snickers fiancée?" I asked with a straight face to get my dude all riled up.

"I know what you doing, Nate, and I don't like it." D threw his death glare my way, but that shit never bothered me. He was my little brother, no matter how big he was. I'd seen how protective he was with LaTonya when he brought her home to reunite us with Talley.

LaTonya was perfect for D. She was fiery and she loved his complicated ass beyond his past and his oversexed history. LaTonya was fine, but she wasn't my type. He could sleep easy on that one. *That's because you like five-feet-nothing, petite Zanaé and Veronica built women!*

"You know she bad. I'm just trying to get a hug so I can congratulate her," I kept on.

D stood and grabbed his towel and water bottle. "Fuck you, bro."

"I'm kidding. You know she's not my type, anyway."

"I think I have an idea about your type," D teased as we left the gym for the day.

Four

VERONICA

I'M SUCH A BITCH! *I'm a piece of shit. Nobody likes me. Everybody hates me, and I deserve it. I'm an idiot. He was right. My dad was right about me. I'm worse than him and I hate him. I wish I was someone else. How did I get here?*

This had become my morning ritual since last month. I'd awaken, eyes not yet open, and I'd berate myself for all the horrible shit I'd done. Next, I'd reach for my phone to read the media posts that affirmed my shady character. There was a website devoted to protesting the fact I didn't receive jail time for my crimes. They were right. I deserved to be in prison for violating Nina's privacy.

It was hard to think about the magnitude of what I'd done, so I avoided it. I didn't think about the impact of my actions, just how pitiful I was for existing. I had therapy in an hour and the last thing I wanted was to talk or be seen. I wanted to disappear, but I didn't have the nerve to end my life. I was too exhausted to take any decisive action of that magnitude. I also felt like I deserved to live in pain for the awful decisions I'd made.

I stumbled over the empty pints of ice cream and pizza boxes lined along the floor of my bed. They were accentuated by the crumbled cotton tissue littered across my comforter and floor. I was a mess. I'd waited until the last moment to try to get myself presentable for my mandatory session. I'd sidestepped jail time due to this being my first offense and Nina's refusal to take legal or collegiate action.

I was ordered to do one thousand hours of community service with at-risk girls and to attend counseling sessions once a week until the end of my time at ENEP or whenever the counselor determined I no longer needed the sessions. Not knowing when the counselor would decide we were done, pissed me off. When was the actual end date? Was I going to be in counseling until I graduated?

I threw on Rashad's hoodie and the memory of him brought on a fresh set of tears. I didn't love Rashad, but I knew he loved me. I realized after everything was said and done, he was right. When he confronted me with his roommate and LaTonya, he'd basically said if I loved him, I would release him. He claimed my first response wouldn't have been revenge if I truly cared. I could see it clearer now.

Love or not, what I missed was his presence and concern for me. But now, he was happy with Nina. I knew deep down, he deserved someone who could love him back. I couldn't possibly love him. I had no idea what love was. I didn't even love myself. But the thought of him moving on and not pining for me made something click in me. *Don't go there!*

I stepped into a pair of sweatpants and finger combed my unruly hair. I decided the easiest and quickest thing for my no longer straightened hair was to once again mash it under a NY baseball cap. I knew nothing about the team, or sport, but I sure as hell didn't relish California anymore. The cap was an obvious form of rebellion toward the locals. I wanted to run away but was too lazy to make it happen.

I grabbed my keys, my bag, and my Beta Delta Delta water bottle. I knew better than to carry my Greek paraphernalia, looking the way I did. We were to look pristine from head to toe when we wore our letters; otherwise, we were a misrepresentation of the sorority. I was a disgrace and wasn't sure if I'd be kicked out of the chapter once the news of what I did spread beyond ENEP.

I avoided my reflection in the mirror. I already knew I looked like shit. I'd never ignored my appearance the way I had these last few weeks. *Except for when your dad beat your ass!*

Maybe therapy could help me with my thoughts. I didn't have the energy to fight or correct them. These days, eating and bathing were a huge feat, and sometimes, I only had the will to do one of those.

The exterior of my apartment mirrored the inside. There were newspapers and mail scattered across my small stoop. The leaves of my potted plants were brown, and I was being an awful plant mommy. *Shit. Could this day get any worse?*

"Veronica, Veronica!" someone shouted behind me. It scared the crap out of me. I dropped everything I carried in my hands, including the glass Beta Delta Delta water bottle. It shattered into a million pieces. The shards of glass symbolically reminded me of how messed up my life was.

"You scared the shit out of me," I said aloud this time to whoever she was because I didn't recognize her.

"I'm Reese with the ENEP Student Daily. Are you aware students are signing a petition to have you expelled from ENEP?" Reese asked with her cell phone shoved into my face.

"What?" I was confused. I also felt hungover. I hadn't drunk any alcohol, but I'd spent the entire night, splitting my time between binge watching trash TV and going down rabbit holes on social media.

"Students at ENEP are referring to you as a pedophile."

"Pedophile?" I questioned quietly and more to myself than to Reese.

"Yes. The students feel selling and posting child pornography violates the safety of the student body."

"I didn't sell anything," I said, finally standing and abandoning my glass water bottle; it was gifted to me by one of my favorite sorority sisters. My throat had a giant lump in it, and I worried I would start crying. I quickly put on my large designer sunglasses.

"So you do admit to posting child porn?"

"What? That's not what I said. That's not true." I saw a group of people posted at the end of my driveway. They whispered to each other, and a few had their cameras pointed at me.

"This is private property. I need you to leave," I said to Reese. "And I don't give you permission to video record me." I tried to sound authoritative, but my voice broke.

"Did you get Nina's permission?" one of them yelled. They'd moved closer to where Reese and I stood at my door. I retrieved my keys from where they'd fallen and shuffled over to my car; my heart pounded double time in my chest.

"You should be in jail," another girl sneered. That was when I felt a sudden surge of cold liquid against my profile. One of the students had thrown an iced coffee at me and hit me in the face. I climbed into my car, drenched and sticky from the altercation. I asked if things could get any worse and I'd received my answer within no time.

They gathered beside the window of my Mazda, yelling expletives at me. What if I accidentally hit one of them? I'd certainly go to jail if I did. I cracked the window of my car and loudly demanded they move so I could exit my driveway.

The next thing I knew, someone spat inside of my car. I laid on my horn. I was in a fucked-up position. I'd done some unforgivable shit, but not to them, and the last time I checked, spitting on someone was assault.

"Move, or I will run your asses over!" I screamed at the top of my lungs. They responded by getting the fuck out of the way.

I wanted to go back inside and hide under the covers, but if I didn't drive to the appointment now, I'd be late and in violation of the conditions set by the dean. *Fuck!*

MY FACE WAS STILL sticky from the iced coffee the ENEP student threw at me. The remnants were undeterred by the paper towel I drenched with water from the therapist's waiting area restroom. I'd unsuccessfully scrubbed my tear-stained face and decided my sunglasses and hat would conceal the assault.

I was met by a chipper assistant who quickly delivered stacks of paper on a clipboard.

"Chantel?"

"Veronica, please," I said, ready to go home, and the session hadn't even started.

"Oh, yes, I'll be sure to add you prefer to be called by your middle name. Both are beautiful, by the way," Chipper Face said with a smile I felt was genuine. How were people so damn happy? *I hate happy people.* I snatched the paperwork from her, but she didn't seem to notice. I plopped down in a chair, off to the corner of the room, and hoped I didn't recognize anyone.

I wrote vigorously for fear if I were even a minute late, I'd be punished. It turned out, I had plenty of time to conjure up old ghosts and write about them on the forms. I omitted and lied about a few things, but everybody did, right? *Just you, you shameful bitch!* Maybe this therapist could show me how to change my negative self-talk. *Who am I kidding?*

The assistant with the sunny disposition ushered me into the office for my session ten minutes later. I sat on a comfortable couch positioned across from my counselor's door. The couch's cushions were plush and chunky, but the arms of the furniture were sleek and gave the room a spacious feel.

Her office walls were painted charcoal gray where neatly arranged frames clung to them. The pictures were hung on the wall adjacent to the door. There were three floor-to-ceiling, door-sized windows alongside the door I had my eyes trained on.

I'd filled out all the forms and written my life story between the tiny, sterile lines of the patient history sheets. I prayed the hour would be a general meet and greet and maybe entail a brief discussion of expectations and end with the collection of my paperwork. Those prayers were not answered.

Dr. Emma DeLucchi was an older, Italian woman with an accent that soothed me, even though she wanted to discuss topics that were off limits. She started the session with the most irritating questions, most of which, I responded to with one-word answers.

"Have you had counseling before?"

"No."

"Do you have a family history of mental illness?"

"No." *But my dad is a psycho.*

"How about a history of violence? Were you ever physically abused? Ever become physically abusive when mad?"

"No, no, and yes. I've slapped someone now and again, but everyone does." I lied about the physical abuse questions without batting an eye. I wasn't here for that. And it took a tremendous amount of effort not to roll my eyes at her with the last question.

"Have you thought of harming yourself or ending your life?"

"No." I lied again. I knew I didn't have the guts to go through with it, but I *had* thought about it. Dr. DeLucchi scribbled on her paper and the sound of the pen pressed against the clipboard made me want to slap it out of her hand.

I let my eyes wander and got distracted by a breathtaking orange and brown monarch butterfly. My brain couldn't compute how it was suspended outside the window of her fifteenth-floor workspace. The butterfly flapped its wings but remained at its current altitude. It seemed to remain at a fixed height, eye level with me.

"Unhealthy dependent," Dr. DeLucchi said. Her words regained my attention. I turned in her direction, then back to the window where the butterfly had been. It must have flown away.

"What?" I asked. I wanted to watch a movie. Any romantic comedy could snatch me from this hellish reality called my life. I'd stooped to such a pitiful level, I consumed the trash reality TV I judged other people for watching. But anything that allowed me to observe life without living it would do.

"Have you ever heard of an unhealthy dependent?" she asked in her thick, Italian accent.

"A what?"

"An unhealthy dependent."

"No. Sounds like an independent person to me. What's wrong with that?" I was uncooperative in our conversation, but what did she expect?

"An unhealthy dependent is different from an independent person. An unhealthy dependent is a person who had a childhood that results in an adult who has a dysfunctional relationship with themselves and others. This could mean isolation and denial of physical, emotional, and sexual intimacy or excessive relationships that assist the unhealthy dependent in regulating emotions that should be regulated internally.

"An independent person is the opposite of an unhealthy dependent. An independent person is someone who identifies themselves as separate from external sources—people, places, and things. Does any of this resonate with you?" she asked.

I just stared at her. *Childhood, intimacy, regulating emotions.* This session felt like a master's level course on life. I didn't sign up for a degree in human behavior.

My phone chimed and I instinctually checked my home screen. The ENEP article headline read, *"Campus-wide feminist group obtains over three hundred signatures to have student Veronica Waters removed after serving no time for child pornography charges."*

The article interviewed one of the organizers. Student body president for the Women's Rights organization, Alisha Johnson, says, 'When our safety and privacy are violated in the way Nina Jordan's was, we must act. If violations aren't met with appropriate consequences, we will protest.'

"Veronica?"

Dr. DeLucchi walked over to where I sat trembling, looking at the consequences of my foul behavior. I didn't lock the screen of my phone when she peered over my shoulder to see what had me shook.

"This has no bearing on what happens to you. Do you understand that?"

"Have you ever seen a protest? If enough students make a fuss, the higher ups will make an example out of me," I said as I fought back tears; crying seemed to be my new normal. "I just need to transfer. If I transfer before they expel me, I'll probably have a shot at getting accepted somewhere else."

"Give me another week. If you ultimately decide to transfer schools, it is fine, and honestly, understandable. But what I seek to teach you in our time together is, no matter where you go, there you are. What do I mean by this?

"There is a reason you responded to the situation the way you did. You're an attractive woman, living in California. What would happen if your next love interest were a celebrity? What if the fallout is public? Instead of thousands of students' opinions on your choices, you suddenly have millions of people saying much worse things than a group of motivated students.

"I want you to leave my sessions with the confidence and the tools to face anything that comes your way. With support, of course, but without unhealthy dependence and without a need for escapism.

"I understand I've given you a great deal of information. What are you thinking so far, Veronica?"

"Yes. This is a lot. What exactly do you want me to say?" My eyes watered, but I was confident she couldn't see them through my tinted lenses.

"I want you to consider if the definition of an unhealthy dependent might explain some of the recent events you've experienced during your time at ENEP. There is a group dedicated to the discussion of unhealthy dependency, who meet several times each week on campus. I highly recommend them.

"I suggest you attend a meeting before our next session. They will also share more information, but from a perspective that mirrors yours. I acknowledge the work we do together will be one-sided.

"I've studied and trained to assist you in identifying which areas of your life aren't working and how to improve. But these students, mostly powerful women, will exchange their own personal and relatable experiences with you," Dr. DeLucchi said like this was an everyday conversation.

She was gentle with her delivery, but I wanted to put her on pause and search YouTube for videos to explain every other word she'd spoken.

"The last thing I advise, which I realize will feel quite counterintuitive, is to practice being gentle with yourself. I don't want to make any assumptions, but my gut is telling me you're probably being quite harsh with how you handle yourself." She checked in with me. I nodded my head slowly.

"While I want you to take this process one day at a time and allow yourself to progress imperfectly, try to cultivate kindness toward yourself. I'm going to send you away with the details for the unhealthy dependent meetings and a list of mantras I want you to repeat daily. Hang them beside your bed or by the mirror in your bathroom. If you want to change your life, you must start with the way you speak to yourself."

"I'll try," I said. My voice cracked. Unshed tears burned in my eyes at the notion that *I* deserved kind words. Dr. DeLucchi must be insane if she thought I was capable of anything but the truth. I was a piece of shit for the things I'd done. I deserved exactly what I got, and it would take a miracle to convince me otherwise. For now, the threat of jail time would have to be my motivator to keep at it.

Dr. DeLucchi stood and motioned for me to follow her to the door.

"I look forward to our session next week. In the beginning, you may struggle to see the validity of my point of view and the reasons for my suggestions. With that being said, you did a lot of work simply showing up today. Allow yourself to rest this evening and drink plenty of water."

I rolled my eyes because I knew she couldn't see them behind my dark lenses. Before I was out of the waiting area, my phone vibrated with two emails from my therapist; details for the campus meetings and affirmations I was to say to myself daily. *Ugh!*

Five

VERONICA

THE MEETINGS DR. DELUCCHI swore by were held in an old building behind the library. I'd never paid much attention to it because I didn't have classes or any other business there. I wore what had come to be a uniform of sorts: a hooded sweatshirt and my cap pulled ridiculously low over my eyes. I didn't fucking want to be out of my house, yet I desperately wanted my life to change.

When I arrived at the room indicated in the email, I heard women's voices. The meeting started ten minutes ago, but it wasn't a class, and it wasn't mandated in the terms by the dean, so I genuinely didn't give a fuck about my tardiness.

I opened the door, and it creaked loudly, as if it desperately needed WD-40. *Shit!* Out of the eleven or so girls in attendance, only one looked up when I entered. The leader of the group was seated at the front of the circle; she had everyone else's attention.

As the girl detailed 'how to recover' and how her life improved since she joined the group, I quietly sat in an open chair.

The other girls were beautiful. Some were awkward, but they didn't seem like they had any apparent issues other than the fact they were at this meeting. I'm not entirely sure what I expected them to look like, but they looked normal.

"It's important for us to love ourselves. It's key," the beautiful, thick girl said. It seemed like she'd taken the position to poke fun of us. The energy she gave off felt as though loving herself was second nature.

"Psht," I snarled and rolled my eyes.

"Did you have something to add?" The thick girl turned her body toward me, and I caught a glimpse of her name tag. It read *"Sade"*. Everyone's eyes were on me now and I was certain my neck was red.

"Yes. I don't know if I belong here yet. You said to attend five meetings or so before I decide, but what you're saying is condescending."

"In what way?" she asked with curiosity. I was shocked she wasn't offended by my outburst or my statement.

"If what you mentioned when I walked in is true, I have a self-love deficiency? And based on what you read, I'm probably an unhealthy dependent, like everybody else here. If I'm lacking self-love, I find it quite dismissive for you to tell me to love myself. What even is that?" I pressed as I once again fought back angry tears.

I was convinced I didn't belong in this cultish group, only, the "characteristics" listed on the handout, and what I'd heard so far felt like pages from my journals. If I weren't supposed to be here, I wouldn't be upset. I surely wouldn't be on the verge of tears. I stood abruptly and grabbed my bag.

"Wait. We generally save questions until the end of the meeting, but you're new and you have a very valid concern," Sade insisted. "Does anyone else feel the same way? Is anyone else lost on the practical steps to take toward loving yourself? If so, raise your hand."

One by one, the girls seated in a circle of fold-out, sterile gray chairs raised their hands.

"Those with your hands raised, keep your hand up if this is your first meeting."

All their hands lowered. I snapped my head in her direction to see what the hell her point was. I didn't want to be surrounded by a bunch of losers—girls who were unable to love themselves. Wouldn't they lower my self-esteem? What about birds of a feather?

"I asked the group these questions so you can see we're *all* on a journey of self-discovery. Because of our childhoods and past traumas, we find it difficult to naturally love ourselves.

"I can't give you a step-by-step formula like those Tik Tok and YouTube videos. That shit doesn't work, anyway. I would suggest you do an experiment for one week. Shift all the energy you put toward others—hating your parents, smothering your man, stalking your man, being the counselor in your friend group—and direct a tenth of this energy toward yourself.

"It would be a practical first step in loving yourself. When I started recovery in meetings like this one, I had no idea what I liked. If I weren't buying a gift for a friend, what would I buy for myself? Wouldn't that be selfish?

"If I wasn't watching a movie my boyfriend at the time liked, what would I choose to watch solely based on my interests? That's why unhealthy dependents do recovery just like the drinking program—one day at a time," Sade concluded.

Her words knocked the wind out of me, and I felt... seen. The last thing I wanted in life was to be discovered separate from my curated identity. I felt like I would die from exposure. I hadn't sat while she spoke, so I simply shifted my body and scrambled out of the room without another glance in their direction.

MY THERAPIST WAS on my case about those twelve-step meetings, but that shit was too much. I decided to do it my own way and check out a twelve-step yoga class I saw advertised on a flyer in the student union. At least there wouldn't be talking required. I could move my body and let whatever healing needed to happen occur through movement. I was about to be late to the first class. *Dammit!*

The class was to take place at an off-campus yoga studio called *Synchronicity.* It was a cute setup, I guess. It was arranged to appeal to the new age crowd. I didn't recognize any ENEP students, and I was relieved. I'd never done yoga, but I stretched a lot for cheer and dance so it wouldn't be too far out of my wheelhouse.

When I stepped inside, I felt like I would fall asleep. I was tempted to sit and nap in one of the plush chairs underneath a living tree—planted alongside a wall-length, floor-to-ceiling window—but I was already late for the class I came for. I prayed the teacher wasn't one of those who locked the door at two p.m. on the dot. If he or she did, I was about to be locked out.

The room for the yoga class with the twelve-step focus was labeled *Black Tourmaline*, whatever that meant. I saw people lay their mats out through the cracked door and my shoulders sagged in relief. I grabbed the door handle and pulled it open.

I clapped my hands over my mouth to muffle my scream. The yoga instructor was Nina. *Rashad's Nina.* She stood on the platform beside him, and he had his hand over her small, rounded belly. She glowed like a yoga goddess barbie doll, and he smiled a smile of pride he'd never worn with me. I backed out of the room quietly. *She was pregnant?*

I rushed out of the studio and knocked into a few people in the process. I was on the verge of a meltdown. I made it to the parking lot when I felt my breakfast bubble in my stomach. I ran to the bushes and let my breakfast make its way back up. *Argh!*

"I've heard of smoking and yoga, but I've never heard of drinking and yoga. Rough night? Wait, you're supposed to be on the good girl list." There was a smile in Nate's voice when he spoke.

My head was still down, but I remembered his gruff tone from the Student Rights building and the other day when he invited me to lunch in the student union. *Why me? Bitch, 'cause you deserve this shit. And what you don't deserve is his fine, accomplished ass. You will fuck his life up, just like you did Rashad's.*

"I'm not drunk. I got sick," I responded truthfully.

"Let me help you," Nate insisted. He walked around the bushes from the parking lot of the Law Offices of Tulsa and Osage Avenue, dressed in sweats and a fitted t-shirt. *Double damn, he is fine!*

"No. I'm good. Thanks. This is pretty gross." I was so fucking embarrassed.

"Wait here." He left me by the bushes. Once he stepped away, I tried to push the fly aways from my face and wipe my mouth before he returned. I was a mess, but I didn't have to look like one. I smoothed my clothes one last time before he rejoined me.

"Here," he said as he returned with a cold bottle of water from the front seat of his ebony colored Lincoln Continental. *OK, Big Nate.*

"You carry cold water bottles in your car?" I asked, confused.

"No, pretty lady. I'm the new kid around here with the other lawyers, so I get stuck bringing water or coffee to all the meetings," he explained. His lashes were as long as mine, and I had to fight for my life to focus on his words.

He had a single curly gray hair on the side of his goatee, and I wanted to touch it. I had no idea what was up with me. *You need some dick, that's what's up with you. But you're not getting any with vomit on your breath. Simple ass!*

"Just Veronica."

"Huh?"

"You keep calling me pretty lady. I thought maybe you forgot my name is Veronica."

"Nah, I didn't forget. I actually like your first name. Can I call you Chantel? Anybody else call you Chantel?"

There was no damn reason for him to be this sexy. I'd dated a boat-load of beautiful men in my past, but this one had a body and a face created for the romantic comedies I watched incessantly. His masculine scent assaulted my nose and made my stomach dip for a completely different reason.

"Oh OK. And yes, that's fine. My mom and stepdad call me Chantel," I divulged. Few people knew this about me, but Nate was easy to talk to. I hated when people who didn't know shit about me used my first name. Strangely, I didn't seem to mind if Nate did, especially if he said it like he'd just said it.

Scenes of us in the backseat of his Lincoln crowded my mind. I cleared my throat and dug in my bag for a piece of gum.

"I know you gone share. I just climbed Mount Everest and swam through an ocean of alligators to bring you the cleanest bottle of refreshing water, and you're going to hoard the gum for yourself?" Nate asked, and flirted with me when he did. Why the hell was this beautiful man interested in me? He just saw me vomit in a bush. *Easy. Even lawyers need ass!*

"All you have to do is ask," I said as I handed him a stick of gum. When his long fingers grazed mine, he grasped my hand unnecessarily and inspected them.

"Your hands are the size of a doll. They let you drive with these little ass hands?"

I threw him a side-eye but got a kick out of his playful jab. It felt like grade school when the boys who liked me pulled my pigtails. "My hands aren't that small, Nate. Yours are just freakishly large."

I turned away from him because his gaze was unnerving. He'd stared down at me like he wanted to eat me for lunch, though he tried to play it cool. "And alligators don't live in the ocean," I said under my breath.

"Oh sheesh, is it crocodiles?"

"Maybe you should stick to law, Nathaniel Brown," I threw over my shoulder. I felt my cheeks heat at our banter. How this man was able to get me to smile after the shit I saw inside of the yoga studio was a mystery to me. The thought of *Synchronicity* reminded me why I vomited in the first place.

Nate scratched the back of his head. "You gonna leave me on a cliffhanger?"

"Use google, Nate," I called over my shoulder with one last backward glance. I wanted to stay and talk, but I couldn't risk another glimpse of a pregnant Nina and a proud Rashad.

Six

NATE

I'D FINALLY GOTTEN around to the grocery store and went about the business of cooking a meal in my new place. I relished the process of meal preparation because it felt meditative and peaceful for me. I could process the day or past events without interruption. As I chopped scallions, I thought about how my first few classes as a visiting professor at ENEP had gone well.

I'd never officially taught, but I'd done a ton of successful study groups. I was a natural teacher because I loved to learn. The best way to retain information was to explain it to someone else.

The ENEP students in my intro to law course were inspired to hear from someone who hadn't been in the practice of law for decades. Most law professors had a gang of time in the game. And though they'd experienced a great deal, they were almost detached from the current day-to-day aspects of the profession. It seemed to be more impactful for the students to speak to someone with experience, yet whose career could unfold before them in real time.

Veronica had been on my mind since she rejected my offer to have lunch with me last week at the student union. Then I ran into her again yesterday when she got sick outside of the yoga studio, and it only amplified my curiosity. I wondered if she was hungover and who she had gotten drunk with.

I needed to know if Ms. Chantel Veronica had a man. If she had one, he didn't seem to have her full attention. I knew she wanted me, or at the very least, was intrigued because she'd watched my lips when I spoke to her. Unless she struggled with her hearing and read lips during conversations, she was attracted to me, too.

I put my meal in the oven and dialed her number. I didn't press send, though. I had no business with her number in the first place; I got it from her student file. This officially crossed the line. It would be much more appropriate to let her give it to me before I called. I was better than this and I knew to get her consent first.

Hours went by and I enjoyed the fresh food and a single serving brownie dessert I bought while I was out. I wondered what Veronica was up to for the night. I wanted her around me and in my home. I was a mellow person by nature, but I sensed a woman like Veronica would bring life and adventure to my mostly quiet life.

I sat upright in bed and gazed over at my alarm clock. It was eleven-thirty p.m. If I was going to call her, I needed to do it now before it was the official hit you up to Netflix and chill hour. I dialed her number from the comfort of my bed because I'd memorized it after the first time I saw it.

"Hello?" Veronica answered. Her voice tickled my ear through the phone, and my body tightened in response.

"Yeah, Veronica?" I didn't know why I asked. I knew it was her.

"Yes. Nathaniel Brown?"

Well, damn. She knew who I was from two spoken words? I smiled brightly and ran my hand down my bare chest. "Yes, ma'am. Did I catch you at a bad time?"

"It depends. Is this about ENEP?" She sounded a contradictory mixture of amused and hesitant. I heard the apprehensive smile in her voice.

"Unfortunately, no. I did not call about anything related to ENEP. Is it OK that I hit you up?" I held my breath for her response.

She giggled. The sound of her laughter felt like a warm hug. She didn't seem like she laughed enough, and though I couldn't fully be sure, I didn't think she'd laughed *at* me. "I guess I'm OK with it. You're kind of a boy scout, Nathaniel Brown."

I liked how she said my name, shit. "OK, good. I try to abide by most laws."

"Most?"

Veronica was sassy, and I couldn't believe how much it turned me on. In the past, a woman with even a hint of an attitude gave me a headache. The aggression felt unnecessary, and I'd preferred someone docile and sweet. There wasn't shit docile or sweet about this girl.

"Well, yeah. I abide by the ones that make the most sense. I wanted to talk to you, but the rule of waiting for you to give me your number would have taken too long," I admitted.

"What about the fact that you're a whole lawyer and professor? Technically, this is fraternization. Will you get in trouble or break any rules, flirting with me like this?" she purred. I had to fight not to slip my hands down my drawstring. This girl was dangerous.

I cleared my throat. "Who said I was flirting?"

"You're definitely flirting. You're not even sitting upright. I imagine this is late for you because you're kind of an old man. Let me guess, you're in bed, half-dressed with a fancy goblet of wine on your end table."

"Shit." Her laughter danced through the phone and the sensual inflections from her voice traveled to my ear and my dick at the same time. "I'm twenty-five." I wanted to put it out there quickly. "I'm not old. We can't be more than five or six years apart. How old are you?"

"You have my file, Professor Brown. You know how old I am and probably my zodiac sign. Are we compatible or nah?"

I choked on the wine she so eloquently called me out for.

"Are you OK?" Veronica sounded concerned and I found it cute. I did choke hard as hell because I was the one who normally read people, not the other way around. There was also something about the way she said professor that made my pulse accelerate.

"I'm good. You just ain't have to put me on blast like that."

She breathed a sigh of relief. "I was giving it to you straight. And I'm twenty years old. Now, you answer my question."

"I like the way you say Professor Brown." I didn't intend to say what

I thought aloud. I quickly continued, "And what question?" Though I knew damn well what she'd asked.

"I like when I say it, too. And you know what question, but since you almost died from the shock of my directness, I'll ask you again. When is my birthday, and are our zodiacs compatible?"

"June 13th is your bornday, and a Gemini woman is quite compatible with a Libra man." I heard her intake of air and I wanted to see her full lips do the shit in person. "You there?"

"Yeah," she breathed.

"What's up? You got beef with Libra men or something?"

"No. Not at all."

Silence stretched between us for several minutes, but neither of us seemed to mind. I listened to her breathe and didn't feel weird about it at all. I felt like the quiet was as much of a conversation as the words.

I ASKED her about her time at ENEP before everything went down with her ex. I also asked about her sorority and what made her join. She was open and I felt I'd gotten to know her better in a short amount of time. Veronica asked me if I always wanted to be a professor, to which I responded no and promptly changed the subject. I couldn't handle the word 'professor' from her mouth at this hour.

"Can I see you again? I mean, not now, but for lunch. Since you shot me down last time, I thought maybe you had a man." Her mischievous laugh gave me pause. I'd assumed she didn't have a boyfriend without asking her first. "Are you seeing anybody?"

"Yes and no."

"So, you're in a situation? I don't want to step on anybody's toes. I'd hate to hurt buddy's feelings and all."

"Really? How would you do that?" She flirted with me, and it turned me on. I wasn't thrilled she hadn't fully divulged whether she was involved, but at this point, I didn't care. I would have her, whether there was someone else in the picture or not.

"You're interested in me. I don't know where that leaves the other guy you're dealing with."

"You're just going to tell me I'm interested in you?"

"Are you? Interested in me, Chantel?"

I heard her swallow hard, and I got the feeling Veronica liked when I called her by her first name. Duly noted.

"I guess we'll have to see. It's getting late, though, and I'd hate to have you miss your morning run or hike or whatever old men do to stay in shape for young women."

I roared with laughter and heard her join me.

"Damn, it's like that? Why I gotta be old? And it's not that late, it's only..." I looked back at my alarm clock, and it was a few minutes 'til midnight. She was right. It had gotten late, but I was nowhere near ready to end my time with her. "OK, shit, it is late. Before I let you go, I'm gonna need to know if I can meet you for lunch, and if you have a man."

She didn't respond right away, and I wondered if she fell asleep.

"I'm not seeing anyone, Nate. You know more than most, my life is a bit of a mess right now. And unfortunately, I can't do lunch tomorrow."

"Oh OK. I can give you space. I didn't mean to—"

"Look, I want to go out with you, but I have community service tomorrow. It's first thing in the morning, for me at least, and runs through a proper lunch time."

"I see. Well, I'll let you get your beauty rest. Is it OK if I call you again?"

"Yes, Nathaniel Brown. You can call or text me anytime you get the urge."

"Shit, OK. Sweet dreams, Chantel Veronica."

"Goodnight, old man." I laughed as I disconnected the call. I stood from my bed and ambled to my bathroom to take a much-needed cold shower.

I FELT like I had five jobs here on the West coast. Along with the intro to law class, I consulted with Student Rights and Conduct, I served as special assistant to President Reed at ENEP, and I supported the local law offices of Tulsa and Osage Avenue. I'd been the other lawyers' flunky because I didn't officially work there as an attorney.

They'd been kind enough to let me tag along and get a feel for California law and proceedings. I'd set up the arrangement in the event I wanted to make the move permanent and study for a shortened bar exam to practice law in a new state.

When one of the owners told me I got a message from Zanaé's team, I brushed him off and assumed it was their way of hazing me because I was new. I'd been tasked with coffee and lunch orders from day one, despite the presence of both paralegals and legal assistants. I took it all in stride because I'd been through much worse in my short career. This was child's play and reeked of jealousy.

The owners were the type of attorneys who weren't comfortable with newbies who didn't wear the stress from the job on their faces. It was as if they felt it meant I wasn't learning or working. I got overwhelmed, but I didn't feel the need to talk about it. I breathed through that shit and saved it for my workouts. One of them caught me on Zanaé's TikTok account and never let me forget it. He went on and on about how he should have his niece call me so we could debate which Zanaé song was our favorite.

I learned quickly the message wasn't a joke. Apparently, Zanaé's team left several for me once they learned I relocated to California. I took the card, but I didn't call it right away. What the hell was I supposed to say? There's been some sort of misunderstanding. Your fine-as-hell client needs an experienced lawyer who can listen to her concerns without almost shooting off in his pants.

When I found the balls to make the call, I would likely recommend my mentor, depending on what she needed assistance with. Zanaé couldn't possibly need a civil rights lawyer. If I had to bet money, I'd say she needed the expertise of an intellectual property lawyer, with her rich ass.

I was tight and overwhelmed, so I left the law office for the day to relax. I took my Lincoln for a cruise down Sunset. It was once again some shit I'd seen on TV and wanted to experience for myself. Sunset Boulevard was touristy. While I enjoyed the palm trees and the immense sunshine, I struggled to look past the rampant homelessness. I drove thirty minutes in stressful traffic to get my ass back across the city to my house. I would call my little sister once I got settled. I missed her and my parents.

I arrived home and parked my car in my driveway. I loosened my tie as I leisurely exited my car. I waved at an older, married woman who almost dropped her belongings when she ran out of the house to greet me. I held my laughter until I was safely behind my locked front door. I guess the desperate housewife trope was a real thing.

I changed out of my business casual clothes and into a pair of shorts and a t-shirt. The weather was always nice here, even when the breeze from the water drifted into my villa. I opened the patio doors and took a seat on the bottom stair. I placed my bare feet in the sand and dialed my baby sister.

Her stunning chestnut skin illuminated the screen when she accepted my FaceTime call. She looked cold and I couldn't help but laugh.

"NaTalley!" I yelled delightfully.

"Nate the Great! I hate you for calling me from the beach." She rolled her eyes as she stood in a cream-colored winter hat with a furry ball at the top. I missed her, and just as we'd reconnected, I moved.

I was torn about the decision to move as it pertained to my baby sister. I felt I needed to make up for lost time. In the end, she was one of my main cheerleaders for giving Cali a shot. I'd offhandedly mentioned how D sent me the open position to her and the excitement that covered her face was priceless. She insisted we had our entire lives to be attached at the hip as she so lovingly put it. Talley said she only wanted me to be happy and that I'd worried about her long enough. Between D and me, she felt we deserved all the happiness we could get after over a decade of sadness.

"Well, this isn't *the* beach. It's where I live now." I flipped the screen so she could see my surroundings.

"It is a beach, Nate. And you live there?"

"Yeah, sassy ass."

"That's not fair." Talley pouted. Her doe eyes were big and bright, despite all she'd been through.

"I want you to visit me. D's close and would love to see you, plus I have an extra bedroom. Just send me the dates and I'll fly you out." She squealed loudly. "Does your wailing mean you'll come?"

"Yes! I thought you showed me your place to tease me. If you're asking me to visit, my question is, how soon can I come?"

"You can come today, baby girl. I need to hug you in person."

"I love you!" There was movement and muffled voices in her background. "Mom and Dad want to say hi." Anytime I heard Talley call them Mom and Dad, my heart swelled. Since our reunion, she visited them weekly, and they'd all been closer than ever.

"Son, you look old. I think you have more gray hairs than me," my dad, Nelson, boomed into the phone. Unlike mine, his hair was completely gray. He wore it well, though. My mom called him her silver fox.

"Thanks, dad. How's the weather?"

"You think you're funny. I love my city and the cold weather," he lied.

"Give me this phone so I can see my favorite son," my mother, Nicole, inserted. Her face softened, and since Talley had reentered our lives, I swear she'd aged backward.

"Hey, Mrs. Brown. You found yourself a younger man yet? You're way too fine to be married to a man with gray hair."

"Watch your mouth, boy!" my dad yelled from the background. I saw him search for the glasses already on his head. The sight made me miss them all the more.

"Hey, mom. I want Talley to visit, OK?"

"I know. She's beside herself and talking to one of her friends on the phone about visiting Demetrius and her older brother in California." My mom sighed. She knew Talley was an adult, but I got the impression she wanted her around as much as she could with all the time we'd lost with her. "Watch out for her while she's there. She's so innocent, and those crazy people out there will smell it a mile away."

"It's not like that where I am, mom. If anything, the biggest concern will be the athletes and fraternity members interested in the girl from out of town."

"Did you say fraternity?" Talley pushed her peanut head into the screen with a hopeful grin.

"Ugh, Talley. Don't make me have to break somebody's neck. Matter of fact, I won't have to. D ain't gonna let nobody talk to you." I laughed loudly at the fall in her expression. She and I both knew D wouldn't let Talley out of his sight as far as men on campus were concerned. "Text me the dates when we hang up. I'll get your ticket and see your big head soon."

"Alright, Nate," she said brightly.

"Bye, son," my mom and dad sang together.

"Bye, mom, old man. I love y'all, and I'll talk to you soon.

Seven

VERONICA

I RE-ENTERED the recovery room for the unhealthy dependents meeting, full of shame. I sat, still in shock from how deeply affected I was to discover Rashad would be a father. What stung the most was how happy he looked. If I'd gotten pregnant, I didn't think he would have been proud. He was a good guy, so I think he would have done "the right thing" and tried to marry me, but a merciful relationship didn't feel like enough for me anymore. I wanted to be chosen.

I wanted to be sought after and, if I got pregnant, I wanted the father to look at me the way Rashad looked at Nina. Angry tears crowded my eyes as I tried to force those obsessive thoughts from my mind. *Since when do I cry?*

I always got what I wanted. I used what I had to get what I wanted, but look where it landed me. I was in a room full of weirdos, who acted like they were alcoholics, but they didn't have a drinking problem. *Bitch, your crazy ass belongs right here with them!*

My mind somehow drifted to thoughts of the visiting professor. Big Nate was fine as hell and interested in me, despite his knowledge of what I'd done and his random witness to my public upchuck. *I bet he'd be a good dad.* Where the hell did that come from?

I didn't even want kids, but I was discombobulated over the fact that my ex and his girlfriend would have one. I'd tried to rip them apart and now they shared the ultimate bond. What I couldn't understand was why it bothered me. I didn't love him like I initially assumed I did. Yet, here I was.

"You wanna help me with some chairs, or are you just gonna dehydrate yourself crying?" Sade asked. Her words snapped me from my trance. I'd slipped so deeply into my own thoughts, I hadn't noticed the meeting was over and everyone else had cleared the room.

"Oh, sorry." I sighed.

"Don't be. I've been where you are. Boyfriend cheat on you?"

I said nothing. How the hell was I supposed to answer this? Between the Student Conduct Committee, Dr. DeLucchi, and even Nate, I felt wide open. I wanted to pull a cozy blanket over my head and hide.

"There's no judgment here if you want to talk about it."

"No. I wasn't cheated on. I cheated on him." I was ashamed to admit it directly, especially since Rashad hadn't deserved it. "Then I stalked him and his new girlfriend and posted an intimate moment between the two of them on the internet. How could I possibly be worthy of love?" My insides churned and I got a sensation like I'd regurgitate once again. I wasn't used to vulnerability. It felt anti-bad bitch, in my opinion. This girl would probably roast the shit out of me.

"Whew." Sade blew out a breath and took a seat in the chair beside me. "That's tough. But no matter what we've done, we're still loveable. Because love isn't something that can be lost or earned."

"Do you always talk in riddles? I mean, what does that even mean? I fucking hate myself for what I did. Neither of them deserved what I did to them. Not Rashad and not his annoyingly beautiful girlfriend," I continued.

"I don't always speak in riddles, and I hated when my sponsor spoke this way in the beginning. I yelled at her, too," Sade said calmly with a smirk on her face.

"Huh?" I wiped my face with a crumbled piece of tissue from my bag. Tears leaked from my eyes as I continued to take accountability for my actions. "You don't look capable of yelling."

"Oh, believe me, I did. But unlike you, I yelled *and* threw something. I'm a student, too, and I've only been in this group for a year. I still struggle with loving myself, but my life and the way I look at myself is completely different."

"How did you do it? I mean, I feel like a monster. If I wasn't so lazy and unmotivated, I probably would have taken my life," I admitted quietly.

"I'm glad you didn't. Those of us who experience the type of pain you're describing help the most people. You don't have to figure all of this out tonight. Keep coming back to meetings and you'll hear me share my story in a few weeks. If you stick with this program, you start to rely on a power greater than you, and you get to make amends to those you've hurt."

"You want me to apologize to Rashad?" I stiffened.

"Maybe. If it's safe to do so. But Rashad and the new girlfriend aren't the first people you apologize to," she said as she rubbed my back and stood.

"Who do I apologize to first? My teachers?" I asked genuinely.

"No. The first person you apologize to... is yourself. And don't worry, I belong here, too. My story is pretty intense because I haven't always been calm. I threatened to shoot my stepfather's dick off after my little sister told me he tried to touch her." My eyes got big. "I kept the anger I cultivated for him bottled up inside. Not only did I hurt others with my blow ups, but I also started hurting myself. See you next time, Veronica."

AS PER USUAL, I couldn't sleep. I tossed and turned and found myself engrossed in a chilly thriller flick about a home invasion which took place in the Deep South. The family was in the small town for a visit. They were eventually rescued after over an hour of terror. The teen daughter shared her location via text with her boyfriend, who promptly alerted authorities.

It made no sense for me to watch something so unsettling late at night. I already had trouble with insomnia and nightmares. I slept best with another person in the house or my bed. Unfortunately, it was two a.m., and I was alone. The movie credits were the last thing I remembered before I drifted into a deep sleep and a lifelike, hellish nightmare.

"RONNIE!" *my father yelled. I wasn't in my apartment anymore; I was in the home I grew up in. I watched as the eight-year-old me shook at the sound of my name.*

"Yeah." My young face appeared terrified, and I wanted to look away from the scene, but I couldn't. I was fully aware this was a dream, but could not wake up. I stood and watched as my eight-year-old self slowly went to see what he wanted.

He abused me. I couldn't stomach the idea of seeing it play out this way. Usually, I was eight years old in my nightmares. I would experience the abuse again as if it were the first time. Now, however, I was my adult self in physical form. I was a spectator of my childhood in a way that sent chills down my spine. I'd watch a marathon of thriller and horror films before I'd choose to watch this. Yet, here I stood.

My room was full of the dolls I begged my mom to buy me. They were brown collectibles dressed in occupational outfits. They weren't intended for play, but I played with them as gently as I could and returned them to their rightful box at the end of each night.

Ballerina dolly. I froze at the sight of ballerina dolly. This was the afternoon he broke my arm. He justified it because he didn't actually hit me. He pushed me, then I fell into our living room table and broke my left arm. My arm suddenly ached as my dad yelled at little me. I remembered this fight. He said I ate the last cookie, but I didn't. I didn't like peanut butter cookies.

"I couldn't have eaten it because I don't like what you like," eight-year-old Veronica with the pigtails asserted.

My stomach churned. This was the first time I'd talked back with conviction in my voice. I meant to say I didn't like peanut butter, but I didn't know how.

I quickly ran from my bedroom to the kitchen. The layout was just as I remembered. The smell of his aftershave made me dry heave.

"Leave her alone!" I yelled. But he couldn't hear me. I was translucent and he passed through me like I was a ghost. What the fuck am I supposed

to do here? I can't watch her get pushed! I felt an urge to go to her, my younger self. I tried to hug her, but she flew from the kitchen, into the living room, and crashed into the table. The glass shattered. Somehow, there were no cuts, just one broken bone.

"Make this stop, please!" I yelled. I had no idea who the hell I spoke to. The two of them couldn't hear me. "I fucking hate you, Darnell!" I screamed as he stood, dumbfounded. He regarded my child self with his eyes bulged. He looked... remorseful. I'd never seen him regret any of the beatings he gave me. I couldn't breathe and I needed to get out. This was too much for me.

I SHOT up in my bed as my chest lifted and lowered rapidly. My breath was labored; my brow was damp with perspiration. The dream was over in a matter of hours, but it felt like a lifetime passed. I was dehydrated, and I wanted to find my dad and kick his ass.

"She didn't deserve it," I heaved. "I... I didn't deserve any of it."

THE NEXT MORNING, I felt hungover. I didn't drink any wine, but the recollection of my lucid dream, along with the fact I hadn't drunk water in days, had me disoriented. I lifted abruptly in bed and immediately regretted it. I clutched the side of my head and cursed the bright light dispersed throughout my cluttered bedroom. I was convinced I'd lost my mind.

The memories of last night's nightmare swarmed my thoughts and had me twisted in knots. An unexplainable fire rose in my belly. It reminded me of something I heard in one of those meetings. After a rock bottom, like a Phoenix, the bad shit was burned off. Last night was hell for me, but unlike the dream-like hallucination, I was a grown ass woman now. I was in charge.

I found the nearest water bottle and emptied it. As I felt strong enough to lift from my bed, I stumbled over piles of unwashed or unfolded laundry and made my way to the kitchen for more water. I ate some waffles from a Tupperware lid since none of my dishes were cleaned. My apartment had never been this grimy. It reflected my inner world, and I was ready to change it. I started to sing and clean.

I folded old pizza boxes and recycled them with the empty paper towel rolls. I stacked my dishes in the sink and thought it best to soak them before I loaded them into the dishwasher. As I cleared my counter-tops and kitchen table, my mind drifted to Nate.

Big Nate seemed fascinated with me. He asked me to accompany him while he ate his lunch and I hated myself for being banned from campus dining. He'd asked again, but community service cockblocked his best efforts.

What did a man like him want with a bitchy young chick like me? I didn't care what my inner voice said; I let my mind wander about the possibility of me and Nate. I swept and mopped my floors and made my way back to my bedroom. I gathered my linens and sorted the piles of laundry to be washed.

Nate was tall, smart, and chocolate. It was a deadly trifecta, as far as I was concerned. He was my type, but much more mature than any other guy I'd dated. I longed to be around him, to share his space and his company.

Was it wrong to want to get to know a professor on a personal level? I was in enough trouble already. What if I put him in some sort of trouble? I knew how tempting I could be with men. I didn't want to seduce Nathaniel Brown; I wanted him to come to me of his own accord. A bit of innocent flirting would still be fine, though.

I cleaned from my bedroom to my bathroom and my mood lifted. I cleared and wiped down my sink and caught a glimpse of my reflection in the mirror. My face hadn't aged, and my hair had been the same length since as far back as I could remember. I felt an extreme impulse to cut it.

My hair was part of my pretty girl persona. I played the fair-skinned with long hair card to my advantage. It got me attention from men, and at times, negative attention from other women. But I was in charge now. I wasn't a little girl who needed to play the victim or a role to keep anybody else comfortable. This was my life, dammit, and I only got one.

I rummaged through my drawers until I found it. The shears I used to cut my bangs from time to time after I had a failed salon visit—like the one where the lady cut them too short. I took my jet-black hair down from the messy bun atop my head, held the thick strands in one hand, and with the other, cut my long ponytail at the nape of my neck.

Dark tendrils fell to the floor at my feet and a weight lifted from me. I thought I'd immediately regret it, but I didn't. I wanted the heaviness of the past month or so gone, and a clean house and new hair were a wonderful start to the process.

"VERONICA, what the hell is wrong with you? This is not TV. You can't just grow your hair back because you changed your mind," Lisa yelled. Lisa was my stereotypical, slutty sorority sister. We became friends before we joined the Beta Delta Delta organization. She randomly approached me freshman year and told me I would be her bestie because I looked like a bad bitch, just like her. There was never any real depth to our relationship and that was precisely how I'd wanted it.

Lisa was physically stunning. She was thick in all the right places, had light eyes, piercings, and the swag to match. I'd never been threatened by her, even after I found out she fucked Rashad. I was more upset with him about it. He did it out of retaliation and she was shallow enough to go through with it.

In all the time I'd known Lisa, she'd continually put herself in situations where others alienated her because of her sexcapades. It didn't bother me too much because I was smart enough not to expect anything from her.

I was hella irritated, though. We hadn't hashed things out since everything went down and I had a sneaky suspicion this tramp would try to act like the shit never happened. The least she could do was acknowledge it.

She'd walked into my bathroom shortly after I'd cut most of the length from my hair. I'd hoped I had a pair of clippers because what I really wanted was an official big chop to go along with this fresh start.

And when the hell did Lisa come into my apartment?

I stood at the vanity in my bathroom with scissors and about fourteen of the sixteen inches of jet-black hair on the floor. The shortest I'd ever worn my hair was at my jawline, but I'd cut well past that point and was on my way to a pixie if Lisa hadn't barged in.

Lisa had immaculate hair. Her large, curly afro was as seductive as she was. I was tired of my long, straight, boring hair and my problematic behavior. I guess I hoped if I cut it off, some of my flaws would go with it.

"You got your damn nerves, coming up in my spot like nothing happened," I said as I rolled my eyes. Lisa was "friendly", and everybody knew it. It was unfair to expect her to be anything more than she was. *Bless her heart.*

"V, are you still mad about Raheem?"

"Rashad."

Her face contorted as she questioned, "You sure?"

"Bitch, I think I remember. And no, I'm not mad about him. You shady as hell, but I already know how you roll."

"Oh, thank God. I thought you was gonna try to kick me out," Lisa responded as if she had no problem with the label "shady".

"I think I fucked my hair up," I said, panicked. "What did I do?" My voice was loud and shrill.

The style hadn't come out like I pictured in my mind. Some of my hair was straight and parts had soft curls. My hair looked like it was in a fight with itself.

The freedom of the experience was quickly replaced with dread. All I could think was how Nate wouldn't be interested in me without my straight hair. Maybe I wasn't attractive without it.

"OK, look, V, your face is still pretty as fuck. I'ma take you to my homegirl and she'll do somethin' with it. She gone have you lookin' like you did this shit on purpose."

"Fine! Your treat," I relented.

"It's the least I can do after Rakim," Lisa said with a straight face.

"Bitch, you know damn well I ain't kicked it with nobody named Rakim." I laughed.

"My bad. I'm so silly. It's the least I can do after *Raheem*," she said and emphasized Raheem.

"Bitch."

"Y'all was broke up?" She'd made the statement sound like a question. All I knew was she'd have a black eye if she even looked twice at Big Nate. "I came by to check on you and to say I was sorry about..." Her eyes scanned the room as if Rashad's name would come to her.

"Lisa, his name is Rashad." I rolled my eyes and grabbed my bag as we left my bathroom.

I threw on my aviators and NY baseball cap. As I put on my shoes, she asked, "You sure that boy's name was Rashad?"

Eight

NATE

I'D STRUCK A FAIRLY decent balance between my ENEP intro to law course and my unpaid position with the Tulsa and Osage law firm. Already, Talley had sent the dates she would come to visit, and I'd purchased her flights right away. I'd hung out with D a few more times since I laid Rashad out in the gym. When I stopped by their apartment, he'd left immediately. I wasn't tripping because I didn't have shit to say to him at this point, and I'd only address it for the sake of D's comfort.

I was at the law offices for the day, despite the undesirable conditions. If I decided to sit for the shortened bar in California, the opportunity to be here would be invaluable, so I had no complaints. I had the end goal in mind and could mostly look beyond the foolishness and politics.

My small desk didn't have a door. They treated me like I hadn't passed the bar or like Ohio law didn't count. I could honestly see why, though. Ohio and California were two totally different monsters. While most of the crime in Ohio was born out of lack of opportunity, folks in survival mode, or young people's boredom, California residents may or may not have a reason for their misconduct at all. If some of the cases I'd seen could talk, I felt they'd say, 'I did it because I felt like it'.

My dated landline rang loudly and startled the shit out of me. I'd pushed an open case file the other lawyers prepared for trial aside and scrolled social media.

"Hello?"

"Nathaniel Brown?" I knew who it was instantly. It was Zanaé's publicist. He always had an attitude when it came to his impatience with me.

"This is he."

"We've been trying to reach you. You're a very hard man to track down." I got the impression they wanted to speak with me more since I was unavailable. Hollywood shit. The reality was, I hadn't dodged their call intentionally. I didn't know what they wanted, and once I had their contact information, I was intimidated as hell to reach out.

"My apologies. I relocated to the West Coast and only recently settled into my new setup."

"I see. Are you available at the moment? Someone would like to speak to you personally." There was a smirk in his voice now and I choked on my water. I stayed unable to swallow when some highly emotional shit went down. I'd done it in court a time or two and my colleagues never let me live it down.

"Yep. Give me a second." I coughed. My mind swirled. What the hell was I supposed to say? I stood from my chair as if my current position were too relaxed to speak to R&B royalty. *Stop freaking out! He already said she has a man. You're a professional. Just direct her to your mentor without doing something embarrassing.*

"Nate."

She said my name! I'd bet money she smelled good. She sounded so sexy over the phone. I knew I didn't have a chance with Zanaé, and if I was completely honest, I was quite taken with Chantel Veronica. But I wasn't blind. Zanaé was fine, fine.

"Yes." My voice quaked and I hoped she couldn't hear it.

"Finally. I thought maybe you were avoiding me."

"Never that. I told your publicist I just moved and hadn't settled. When the other lawyers gave me your information, I thought maybe they were hazing me."

"And when you found out they weren't?"

Shit! Zanaé left me no damn slack.

"Alright, I avoided making the call. You know who you are. I didn't want to say something unprofessional."

Her laughter was contagious. As popular as she was, I expected her to be much more unapproachable.

"Good, you've loosened up. I like you, Nate, and I think you can help me."

I took several deep breaths. I knew she meant she liked me in a 'you're a cool person' kind of way, but my body had a mind of its own.

"Yes, about that. I think you're looking for an intellectual property lawyer. I got decent grades and some national-level awards, but my focus has always been civil rights. I don't have any experience with entertainers."

"You're too humble. I've seen your grades and I couldn't find anything lower than an A."

Damn!

"I need your expertise because my civil rights were violated. I don't want a lot of press, but something needs to happen."

"OK. How can I help?"

"Well, I'd like to speak to you face to face, if possible."

I coughed uncontrollably again. One of the old ass lawyers shook his head as he walked by. I must have looked like an idiot.

"OK."

"Are you sure you're OK? Your assistant said you're prone to fainting, and you've had at least two coughing fits."

I laughed and she joined me.

"I'm good. I'm not used to consulting with someone so..."

"Famous?"

"Famous. Or young. Or fine, shit! But I'm normally much more professional. The thought of seeing you face to face again sent the water straight to my lungs." We laughed again.

"How about online? Can you handle seeing me on your screen?"

This time, I swiped the water bottle off my desk and into the trash bin. I wasn't about to choke a third time.

"Yes. When?"

"Now, if you're available. It shouldn't take long."

"OK."

"I'll have Anton, my publicist, send you the secure link and we'll chat."

Less than five minutes later, my phone chimed with a link from a phone number I didn't recognize. I grabbed my laptop and rushed through the front door of the building to my Lincoln so I could have complete privacy for the call.

Once I was seated and had my laptop opened, I clicked the link and about fainted when her beautiful face appeared on the screen. It helped that she was with Anton, the publicist, her bodyguard, and a younger man I hadn't seen before.

The third guy I didn't know gave me a nod and said, "Thanks for taking the time to help my girl."

"Absolutely." He had no idea how happy I was to see him. It was as though my mind needed a reason to make her off limits, and he was it. I didn't feel that way about Veronica, though. I'd lay her man out like I did Rashad without a second thought.

"I'll get right to it." She took a deep breath as she recounted her story. "I was so pissed about a guy I was dating at the time, I didn't consider I was in a stuffy, overly priced, and extremely luxurious hotel. My ex had canceled on me at the last minute once again. He was supposed to accompany me to a charity gala. Events like these require a name and plus-one submission well in advance. There were so many other people who could have used the ticket, yet he had the nerve to commit, then say he couldn't make it."

Her man shifted uncomfortably beside her, and I noticed his jaw clench.

"I'd been recording literally all day. I can't be sure of the time, but I know when I left the studio, it was around two a.m. My driver dropped me off and I was checking my voicemail when I entered FéTim. I generally wait for Goliath, my bodyguard, before walking anywhere. Even when I'm entering my own homes. Hearing the story about Willow's stalker had my team shooketh. But the night of the incident, I had so much adrenaline from what I knew was yet another let down, I broke protocol.

"His message said he wasn't gonna make it to my 'thing'. His baby mama was sick and leaving their daughter with him. He claimed he asked his mom if she'd watch her, but she told him it wasn't her baby. He'd left the message nonchalantly, like he was canceling dinner plans and not the biannual charity gala that would put me in the room with numerous endorsement and acting opportunities and a ton of other avenues to build my brand. I'd gone against my better judgment and shared him on my social media.

"Since then, all my interview questions included inquiries about my new guy and when I would introduce him to the public. The gala was my response. After I heard his voicemail, I was mortified. I knew I would look like an idiot if I arrived solo."

Zanaé shifted uncomfortably, and her voice shook. I had no idea what this whole story had to do with me or my knowledge of civil rights violations. Had the ex infringed on her privacy?

She let the gentleman beside her grab her hand as she continued.

"I was so distracted by the voicemail and my exhaustion from the workday, I hadn't paid much attention to my surroundings. I felt an uneasy feeling, so I looked up and my eyes collided with a security guard who was twice my size and my age. Only, instead of feeling safer in his presence, I felt danger."

Anton looked away and the bodyguard cleared his throat. *What the hell was going on?*

"I still had the phone up to my ear because I had another message, but the old guy was asking if I had identification. I was annoyed with him, but I said 'no' out of courtesy.

"Most of the staff had been prepped not to speak to me, let alone ask me to see identification. Besides, Goliath or Anton kept all that for me. I made the mistake of turning my back to the security guard, and that's when his tone completely changed."

There were tears on her cheeks and the guy beside her had his free hand closed tightly in a balled-up fist.

"The guy told me I needed to leave if I couldn't provide him with a reservation or personal identification. He'd spoken to me like I was a criminal." She sniffed. At that point, my knee bounced incessantly.

"I sighed loudly and smacked my lips. I was exhausted. I needed to rest my voice, and now I had to deal with him. My phone started ringing; it was Anton. I picked it up and noticed a white couple entering

FéTim. They were both drunk, belligerent, and laughing loudly. It was disruptive, to say the least. The guy from the couple fell into one of those carts for luggage and the girl was whisper-yelling expletives. I stared at the couple and then the security guard, but he wouldn't move his eyes from me.

"The guy started holding his girlfriend's arm tightly. I couldn't make out exactly what he was saying, but it sounded like he was accusing her of flirting. My gut told me he was two seconds from slapping her. And as if on cue, WHAM, he struck her across the face. I knew better than to intervene. I'm a public figure. Also, I'd read it takes those women seven attempts at leaving before they're finally done."

As pissed as I was on the inside, I was in full on litigator mode. I took mental and actual notes as she spoke. I'd make it my business to move heaven and earth for Zanaé and her loved ones to own whatever trash ass hole-in-the-wall allowed the incident to happen. It was obvious the guard was terse with Zanaé and ignored the belligerent white couple. I kept my mouth shut because I was positive there was more.

"I spoke with Anton as I went to grab my key fob from my back pocket. That's when the guard yelled, 'Put your hands where I can see them'. Only, I was oblivious to the fact he was talking to me, so I kept reaching for my fob. He wanted a reservation or an ID, but the fob was my only physical proof I belonged there.

"Proof, of course, in addition to my two Grammys and fifteen number one crossover hit singles. I do lots of international shows. I've done cameos in videos for rock and emo artists. It's not like I'm only recognizable with R&B and hip hop fans. Basically, white people, young and old, know me, too. I know this because I'm constantly getting approached at brunch in countries like the Czech Republic and other spaces where the locals are only familiar with three black people: Will Smith, Beyoncé, and Zanaé.

"Before I knew what happened, my ears were ringing and my mouth tasted salty because I'd bitten my tongue and it filled with blood. I'm not being dramatic when I say I was suddenly looking down on myself and trying to scream, but no words came out. I had an out-of-body experience.

"He had his knee in my back. I kept thinking he was going to break my back."

Zanaé's guy stood and paced the floor behind them as he yelled, " Fuck!" loudly. It seemed he hadn't heard her recount the story the way she just had. Zanaé wiped her face with her sleeve, and despite Anton's suggestion we take a break, she waved him off and continued.

"He had his big hand spread across the side of my face and pressed it into the cold ground of the lobby's floor. What I couldn't understand was why there wasn't anyone helping me. I scanned the room and noticed the white couple had sobered up. They stood frozen, facing my direction, but they didn't intervene. They recorded me."

Nine

VERONICA

LISA'S FRIEND, Nessa, cursed me out worse than Lisa did. She said I'd basically given myself a big chop, and unless I could wear my natural curls proudly, I'd need to get a custom wig until my hair grew back.

Some of the ones she forced me to try on were cute, but in the end, I decided to wear my short natural curls. Lisa said Nessa would make it look like I'd cut my hair on purpose, and she was right. Once she'd cut all the straight hair I couldn't reach, I looked like a new woman.

My 3C curls were loose, wavy, and jet black. The short hair illuminated my bright skin and dark features. Nessa threaded my eyebrows and scolded me like I was an insolent child. I told her I did my own brows, to which she promptly told me I should never do them again.

My freckles were aglow, and I hadn't seen my hair this way since I was a child. When I was finally old enough to do my own hair, I straightened it. I thought my curls might trigger some painful memories since my childhood was so fucked up, but it didn't. I felt like the real bad bitch I was born to be.

All the shit I did in my first few years at ENEP was because I was hurt and needed to feel better, by any means necessary. I wanted to bounce back, and I was willing to try whatever Dr. DeLucchi suggested. Nowadays, I didn't feel the need to hurt anybody to manifest my happiness. I could be a bad bitch in my own right and my new hair gave me an overwhelming sense I was on my way.

I HAD no idea what I wanted to be when I grew up. I was one of those girls who genuinely felt if I kept myself fine, I'd marry well. I still wanted a zaddy to take care of me, but now I felt obligated to bring more to the table than my looks.

What am I going to do with my life? I don't like anything except singing and dancing. I can't make a living doing that. Because I lacked direction, I found myself in an anthropology course. It made no fucking sense for me to be here; I hated people. The whole point of each lecture was to learn how and why people behaved the way they did.

All the other students sat at the edge of their seats as they asked questions and took notes. Ugh! It was what I got for not paying closer attention to my academic advisor during our meetings to map out the classes I'd take at ENEP.

I loathed this subject, but I'd be stuck here for another eight weeks. I was bored with the instructor, so I texted Nathaniel Brown.

Me: *Professor Brown. How can I get extra credit? *lip bite emoji*

Big Nate: *Dammit girl, you made me spill water on my pants. *sweating laughing emoji*

Me: *Are you sure it's water?*

Big Nate: *Where are you? Aren't you supposed to be working or studying?*

Me: *I don't have a job. I'm trying to bag a professor.*

Big Nate: *LOL, is that right?*

Me: *That's right. *Wink emoji* And yes, I'm in class but listening to this professor is like watching paint dry.*

Big Nate: *Go easy on your instructor. Teaching isn't as easy as it looks.*

Me: *Whatever. I bet everybody gives you their full attention when you teach. Men and women. *Eye roll emoji*

Big Nate: *Blushing emoji*

Me: *You're not going to ask me to lunch again?*

Big Nate: *I don't think my pride can take a third rejection*

Me: *Try again*

I saw the bubbles like he would text back, but they disappeared. My heart sank. Maybe I had no business falling in like with him, anyway. He was a professional who didn't need me as a distraction.

I finished classes for the day and picked up groceries from the store. Since I was banned from campus dining, I wanted to sneak in on the few occasions where it was absolutely necessary, like between a bunch of classes when I couldn't leave campus; today wasn't one of those days. The grocery store was only a minute or so from my apartment, which was convenient.

Now that I'd started to feel better and get my life back, I didn't feel the need to order fast food as much. I unloaded the grocery bags from my car into my place and only saw a few hate letters on the way in. It seemed things with the student body had simmered as far as petitions for me to be removed, but I'd do my best to stay compliant with the dean, regardless. I didn't want to tempt fate.

I liked to cook, but I hated cooking for one; I didn't think it was possible. I loved to see the look on Rashad or my sorority sister's faces when they tasted my food. I learned to cook because I'd read it was another way to keep a man's interest. I rolled my eyes at my own thoughts. *Bitch, you are so basic for that.*

I ignored my spiteful comment and emptied the bags. My mind drifted to Big Nate. I wondered what he was up to. I considered he might be at work, or maybe he'd found someone else to eat with. He was older than me, so I guessed he ate lunch around noon, like most old people. It was two-thirty p.m. and I'd just finished preparing a quick lunch I'd thrown together. I sat down to eat and grabbed my phone. To my delight, he'd sent a message.

Big Nate: *It's too late for lunch*

Me: *I'm having lunch now old man*

Big Nate: *I'm only twenty-five. Everybody I work with makes kid jokes when they see me*

Me: *It's all about perspective I guess*

Big Nate: *I agree*

Me: *What are you doing?*

Big Nate: *I'm texting you*

Me: *I know that. What else? You hanging out with old ladies your own age?*

Big Nate: *It depends*

Me: *On what?*

Big Nate: *Would it make you jealous?*

A phone call interrupted our text conversation. It was Dr. DeLucchi's office. I hadn't scheduled our next appointment and it was the middle of the week. Thank God, she'd called. If I missed a session, she would report my noncompliance to the dean. I needed to focus.

I washed my dishes and pulled out my books and laptop at my kitchen table. I wanted to text Nate, but right now, boys, or old men, would have to wait. My priority was to keep myself in good standing in my classes and with the dean's requirements. I would graduate on time and make myself proud, for once.

LATER THAT EVENING, I'd completed all the tasks I set out to do for the day. I'd caught up on the homework I was behind on, cleaned the second set of dishes I dirtied for dinner, and did a few loads of laundry. Next, I did something I hadn't done in years: I took a bath.

As I sat and soaked, unbothered by the damp curls on my neck, I threw my head back and relaxed. With straightened hair, I rarely took baths; the heat would ruin it. I felt liberated with a wash and go style.

When I was little, I thought those Herbal Essence shampoo commercials were unrealistic. Nobody should sound as though they'd experienced an orgasm from a simple hair wash. Besides, I wanted a real orgasm, not a hair tingling substitute. But as I let the hot water soothe my tense muscles, I moaned audibly, then laughed at the full circle moment from my young perception of those ads.

I'd taken my time when I set up my bath. I had my wooden bath tray and a book I hadn't opened. I had a liter of water handy, and the edge of my tub was littered with candles of all sizes. The lighting was dim, and my golden bath bomb had me covered in luminous body glitter. My phone lit up and I hoped like hell it was the professor.

Big Nate: *You disappeared on me. Is that a yes?*

Me: *Yes about what?*

I scrolled up to his last message and remembered he'd asked if I would be jealous. I'd be green with envy if he were with other women, but I wouldn't admit it to him.

Big Nate: *Me entertaining women my own age*

Me: *Old people* *tongue out laughing emoji

Big Nate: *Keep sticking your tongue out at me and I'll find a good use for it*

Me: *Is that a threat?*

Big Nate: *Nope, it's a promise pretty lady*

My body tingled at his words. I took a big gulp of water and dried my hands so I could continue my banter with Big Nate.

Me: *I like when you use my first name*
What the hell is wrong with you, thirst bucket?

Big Nate: *OK, Chantel. What are you doing? Breaking teenage boys' hearts?*

Me: *No, I'm home alone*

Big Nate: *What?!?! Already? It's only nine p.m.*

Me: *Yes, Professor Brown, I'm home.*

It took him several minutes to reply, and I had no idea why.

Big Nate: *What are you doing?*

Me: *You really wanna know? I don't want you to have a heart attack over there. I already had you choking on your expensive wine.*

Big Nate: *Word? Lol. Yes, I wanna know. What are you doing?*

Me: *Taking a bath*

I saw the bubbles appear and disappear several times before he responded.

Big Nate: *There is nothing I could say that would be an appropriate response. Also, I thought you'd like to know, I just choked on my wine again*

Me: *LOL*

Big Nate: *I gotta go pretty lady Chantel Veronica Waters*

Me: *Talk to you soon Professor Brown*

Ten

VERONICA

FOR THE FIRST time in a long time, I felt inspired to wear something other than sweats and my NY ball cap. I pulled a pine green sundress from the back of my closet to wear to run an errand on campus. I paired it with motif peep toe high heels. The shoes made me feel like an adult, despite my boyish haircut and small frame.

I had no plans, but it was Friday. Maybe something fun would be planned on campus. *Bitch, you know your treacherous ass can't go to shit on campus!* I shrugged dismissively, as if my mind were in the room with me. Dr. DeLucchi told me I should make peace with my inner thoughts. I wasn't sold on it, but I'd noticed I didn't fight them as much. It wasted the little energy I had to get myself motivated to face the day.

I did one last spin in the mirror and was impressed with what I saw. My small frame and short hair were a sensual contrast to my exposed skin and subtle curves. I anticipated how I'd feel if Professor Nathaniel Brown saw me this way. Since I'd met him, he'd only seen me at my worst. I'd been bitchy, rude, and disheveled with each encounter. Today, I had a glow about me and the person I wanted to see most was him.

CAMPUS WAS PACKED. I had no idea what event might be scheduled because I was banned from campus activities and had basically been disconnected from my entire social life. I knew whatever it was, it wasn't a Greek sorority or fraternity event since I still received regular emails from Jess, my sorority's chapter president.

I'd dropped off the form I needed to deliver and wandered aimlessly. I chatted briefly with a few of my line sisters who happened to be on the path of my unknown destination. They said Lisa told them I disfigured myself, but they loved my new hair. We hugged and they assured me they were available whenever I was up for a chat or company. I loved those girls. They were genuine with me, but I'd been so deep in my own shit, I never considered reaching out.

As I made my way through a group of students, I saw D first. He was so damn tall. He was with the girl I'd called a video ho a few months ago when they confronted me with Rashad about the video I posted. I had an overwhelming urge to apologize to her; I needed to make amends. I took a deep breath and approached them.

"Hey, D," I said, genuinely thrilled to see him happy. He looked peaceful with this girl. When I dated Rashad, he always seemed so uptight and agitated.

"V? Is that you? You look good!" Regardless of what went down with Rashad, he felt like family to me.

"Yep, it's me. A lot has changed since I last saw you." LaTonya didn't look mad, but she certainly wasn't interested in what I had to say. Still, I asked her, "What is your name?" She left my hand suspended in the air when I extended it toward her to formally introduce myself.

"What do you want, girl?"

"I want to apologize for calling you a video ho. I didn't know you to speak to you in that kind of way. I was in a dark place. That's not an excuse, but it's true."

"Thanks, V. New hair, new you, nah mean?" D said with a chuckle, though LaTonya remained straight faced.

"I don't accept." LaTonya's tone was even, and her eyes were unimpressed.

"Uh, baby—" D started.

"No. D, it's her right to accept my apology or choose not to. I understand." I deflated, yet I understood her hesitancy.

"I meant to say, I don't accept your *half-ass* apology. You shouldn't even be a student here. How you shook what I consider revenge porn and possible child pornography charges is beyond me. I don't care about you calling me a video ho. I can't get over how you played my girl, Nina. For that shit, you are not forgiven."

She folded her arms across her chest, and the movement made her large breasts jiggle. D's mannish self hadn't changed much because he looked like he wanted to take her home right then.

"Chantel Veronica Waters?" Nate said from behind me. The throaty way he said my name made my heart pick up its pace and my hands perspired.

I whipped around to see him standing there, dressed in a tailored business suit. His masculine scent of sandalwood, mint, and cedar found my nose and had my head spinning. Nate's fade with the sexy patches of gray was freshly manicured and I wondered what his facial hair would feel like between my soft legs. My panties were drenched.

Nate hadn't acknowledged D or LaTonya and said, "You changed your hair!"

I instinctively rubbed my hand over my short curls with a blush.

"I did."

"Nate Dawg!" D announced over the back of my head. "How's the new gig?"

They caught up for a few moments with me awkwardly trying to leave them to finish their conversation.

"I'll see you guys around," I said as I turned to walk away.

"I'll walk you," Nate called after me. "I just need to speak to Professor Thomas. Can you wait for me?"

"Sure," I blushed.

"I'll see you around, D and D's future wifey. Talley is supposed to visit soon. I want to make sure she has a good time. Who knows, maybe we could get her to stay."

D and Nate gripped each other up with a familiar handshake. I didn't know where I should look and felt like I'd intruded on a family moment by being there.

As Nate made his way toward Professor Thomas, D lowered his voice to a deadly tone. "I'm with you and this new V vibe you're giving off. But that man right there is like a brother to me. He's been to hell and back. If you even think about treating him like you did Rashad, I'm gonna let LaTonya kick your ass. Nah mean?" His mug shifted to a charmed smile as he grabbed LaTonya's hand and said, "It was nice seeing you, V."

Dammit! The two of them scared the shit out of me.

THE AFTERNOON SUN lowered in the sky, signaled the beginning of night. The crowds of students thinned, and I'd pulled a book from my bag to sit and read. I knew how long academic types could talk, so I hadn't been impatient when Nate didn't return right away.

I was engulfed in my Afrofuturism fiction storyline and lost track of time, anyway. I felt eyes on me and glanced up to discover Nate's watchful gaze. How long had he been there? I closed my book and stood.

"Don't move on my account. I was enjoying the view." Nate always spoke flirtatiously. What I couldn't figure out was if he was naturally charming or if he legitimately liked me.

I reflexively ran my fingers through the short curls at the back of my neck again.

"I really like your new look."

"Thank you."

"I'll be honest, you were fine before with your baseball hat and sweatshirts, but dressed up, you take my breath away."

I blushed at his words, and I was sure my skin flushed.

"Do you have plans? Actually, I don't give a damn if you do. Cancel your plans if you have any, and have dinner with me."

I stood and considered his words. He wanted to ask me out, whether I had somebody or not. The reality of his boldness made my center pulse.

"OK. I'd love to."

Nate exhaled a sigh of relief as though he'd held his breath as he awaited my response. I didn't know why someone this fine, talented, and successful would be nervous about asking me out.

We walked toward the student parking lot, mostly in silence. Every now and then, he'd catch me with my eyes on his profile as we continued our journey.

"I don't know you, Ms. Chantel V. Waters, but I like you."

His remark felt like a symphony of the most elegant words. I wasn't accustomed to conversation with an older guy. Most of the guys I dated were either obsessed with their situation, fine with me being obsessed with mine, or focused on my looks. Nate spoke to me like we had all the time in the world to get to know each other better.

It made me feel both treasured and impatient. When would the fucking part happen? *You a slut for that one! But I can't blame you, girl.* I chuckled lightly. Had the voice in my head actually said something agreeable?

"What's so funny?" Nate didn't look offended; he seemed amused.

"Oh, nothing."

"Well, whatever has you smiling, I like it. You don't strike me as someone who laughs enough."

"You're quite serious yourself, professor. You seem like someone who needs to loosen up." Nate faltered in his steps and sucked in a breath of air.

"Are you OK?" I asked and turned my body to face him. We stopped at the edge of the parking lot.

"Since I'm admitting all of my likes, I really fucking like when you call me professor and Professor Brown." He ran his long fingers across my nose where the darkest freckles were sprinkled across my face. "It kind of stops me in my tracks."

"Oh."

"And am I really uptight?" He attempted unsuccessfully to slouch, and it made me snicker. Nate was a legal professional through and through. There was a young man hidden inside of him somewhere, but at the surface, was a serious person who likely had to present in this stoic manner to be taken seriously in his profession with his young age.

"I'm gonna follow you home so we can take one car to the restaurant tonight."

"OK." I sort of sang my response because I was unclear about the reason for his instructions.

"Why do you say it like that?" His eyebrows bunched together like I was a riddle he couldn't solve. He was a cute, pensive young man with an old soul. I think that was why I liked to call him an old man.

"I just figured you'd want me to meet you there."

"I'm not a teenager. I'm a grown ass man. I want the lady I'm spending time with next to me. The only place I want to meet you is back at your place so we can drop off your car." Nate's voice was rugged and raspy, contrasting beautifully with his kind eyes. They were full of fire but otherwise pure intentions.

I cleared my throat and used my keys to deactivate my car alarm. "I'll text you my address. I doubt you can keep up with me. I've turned over a new leaf and I've started to follow the rules of ENEP, but I haven't slowed down my speeding. It's a bad habit, I know, but I try not to go too far over the speed limit."

He looked like he wanted to lecture me about my safety or say something in the way of a warning, but I leaned up and kissed him on his cheek. "I'll see you back at my place, Professor Brown." His body stiffened and he briefly closed his eyes. I giggled and went on my way to my car.

Eleven

NATE

I WATCHED her slink from her car to mine and heard myself swallow loudly. *What the hell am I doing?* Whatever it was, I wasn't about to fucking stop.

We rode in a comfortable silence on the drive from her apartment to the city. I chose a fine dining restaurant, one my attorney colleague suggested. I'd mentioned the desire to take someone out the moment I ran into Veronica on campus. I didn't necessarily think it would be her, but I guess on a subconscious level, I was interested in her then.

The other attorney swore Mabella's was an aphrodisiac. He said every time he took someone there, they basically seduced him before they could fully leave the establishment. At the time, I filtered the information because he seemed kind of douchey with his testimonial. But once I saw Veronica with her short hair and her sundress, I immediately thought of Mabella's.

I caught a glimpse of Veronica's expression as I pulled my Lincoln Continental up to the valet of the upscale, patio-style restaurant. She seemed impressed by the place, and it surprised me. I'd gotten the impression she was accustomed to this type of treatment, but from the awe spread across her features, I accepted that may not have been the case after all.

I unbuttoned my blazer and stepped out of the car to greet the valet. I exchanged words with him about my intention for the evening and promptly derailed his attempt to open Veronica's door. She was my date, dammit, and I didn't need any help watching her sexy ass exit my vehicle.

"Nate, I'm not dressed up enough for this. I look a mess," Veronica said as she ran her hands through the back of her short curls. She was accustomed to designer clothes and a full face of makeup. She had on a green sundress and opened-toe high heels. Though she didn't have makeup or those false lashes on, she still looked alluring and edible to me.

Veronica was probably one of the younger patrons, and therefore, as dressed as she needed to be. She wasn't showing unnecessary skin and she wasn't in jeans. Besides, with the money I would spend in Mabella's tonight, there had better not be so much as a sideways glance at my date and her attire, unless it was to admire her perky breasts and stunning face. *Damn, Veronica is fine!*

"You look stunning! You could have worn your NY cap and sweatpants and still been dressed up enough to have dinner here with me. I don't give a shit about these people."

She blushed and rolled her eyes as if I'd said what I said strictly to reassure her. The thing was, I meant that shit. Veronica could have worn an old shirt and tattered, cut-off shorts with flip flops and I would be content to spend time with her in public.

The hostess escorted us past an elegant, ceiling-less structure; it provided an immaculate view of the sunset. I'd requested outdoor seating when I put in the reservation on the way back to Veronica's place to drop off her car. She hadn't lied about speeding when she drove. A couple of times, I had to fight not to call her or chase down a car who'd gotten road rage with the swift way she cut in and out of the lanes.

Mabella's was reservation-only dining, and when I called, the hostess went on and on about how they'd been booked for weeks. I assured her money was no issue for me and we were magically granted a table of my choice. D had warned me about how California operated, and his advice hadn't failed me yet. He also insisted if I were in a tight position to throw around my occupation, but I hoped there was never a situation that called for me to take it there.

The weather was nice and slightly breezy. Veronica's eyes were on the other diners. They were mostly white, and clearly wealthy, but I came from the school of not giving a shit because my money was green, just like theirs. She seemed uncomfortable with the age and race of the other patrons; I could only guess it had something to do with the attention she received.

The older women wore expressions on their faces that were a mixture of envy and disgust. It was obvious to me they were jealous. I couldn't tell if it would keep her from enjoying our time or if she just felt out of her element.

We were seated at a mahogany table with a built-in fire pit in the center. It was encased by fireproof glass. The sleek, ivory chairs surrounding the table were more like home furniture than restaurant-style furnishing. To our left, was a large tree wrapped in white Christmas lights. I noted Veronica's smile when she took it in.

There was an outdoor bar and numerous other options for seating. The area I'd selected felt the most appropriate to get to know someone. I motioned for her to sit and, to her surprise, I took the seat next to her. The table was too large for conversation across a fire pit.

The decor was as provocative as the lady at my side, and I couldn't wait to officially start this impromptu date. Our hostess left us with menus and informed us our waiter or waitress would be with us shortly.

"Do you know what I did? I mean, you must." Veronica hit me with her question the moment the young woman sauntered off.

"Uh, what?"

"You brought me to this super expensive restaurant, knowing I posted child pornography."

I breathed deeply and responded, "What you did was not child pornography."

"Nina wasn't eighteen when I posted it. In the state of California, any images or video of someone under the age of eighteen, engaged in a sexual act, is child pornography."

"OK. Did you know she was a minor?"

"No. But it doesn't matter in the eyes of the law. Come on, Nate, you know this better than anyone." Veronica sounded remorseful for her actions, and somehow, it clouded my normally black and white thinking as it pertained to fairness and justice. "It's a felony and I should have gone to jail." She beat herself up for what she did, and it made me uneasy.

"I see someone's been on Google." She smiled briefly and used her hand to push me playfully in the chest. I grabbed her hand gently and kept it there as I spoke. "You'd have to have known she was underage and posted the video with the intent of doing so *because* she was underage.

"It was clear your intentions were to intervene in a relationship between your ex and his new girlfriend. An attorney would have a hell of a time proving a student—from the same school as the victim—was guilty of child pornography, especially students of the same gender. Trust me."

There was quiet between us, and I felt she needed the silence. I hoped she would take my words to heart. She reclaimed her hand, and I missed it immediately.

"What if it were your sister?" she asked, barely above a whisper. I opened my mouth, but no words came out. "Would you use the same consideration if Nina was your sister?"

Damn. The truth of the situation was, hell no, I wouldn't, but she didn't need to hear that. I had no idea why I felt immense empathy and attraction toward Chantel V. Waters. I didn't know anything about her other than she'd done a foul thing she felt sorry for, and she was fine as hell.

I knew enough to know her life was complicated long before Rashad and Nina. I saw the pain in her eyes and found it familiar, as it seemed to mirror mine. I spent my young life and profession focused on the pain in others to avoid my own; relationships never seemed possible before now. I feared they'd rip me wide open and reveal the trauma I hid from. Yet, I found myself intrigued with Veronica.

"I like you, Veronica." It seemed like I said it out of nowhere.

"Yeah, I know. You've mentioned that."

Now I had a dumb grin on my face. She was confident, despite her recent indiscretions, and it turned me on.

"Can I get to know more about you, now that we've gotten your ENEP affairs out of the way?"

"Have we? Can't you get in trouble? Your name is on my case. It's got to be a conflict of interest or something?"

"Shit. How the hell do you know so much about the law?" I rubbed the back of my head. I didn't need any trouble with ENEP. President Reed had been good to me. I thought about meeting with him to tell him about my situationship with Veronica before he could hear it from someone else. I just wanted to play my cards right. I hadn't been sure if there was anything between us until now.

"I told you I was trying to bag a professor. And you, Professor Brown, study the law. Why shouldn't I be familiar with it?" she purred.

"Shit," I said again because... shit.

She giggled and I liked the way the sound made me feel. I scooted my chair close to hers and ran my hand across her nose.

"I have never been with a black girl with freckles."

"You still haven't answered my question, professor." Every time she called me professor or Professor Brown, my dick jumped. I thought I liked to hear her call me Nathaniel Brown, but shit. It was something about my name in her mouth that had me ready to take her back to my place, dinner be damned. I shifted in my chair, and she noticed.

She leaned in close to me and I held my breath. "I think I need detention, professor. What can I do to ensure I'm in good standing with you?" I'd be damned if I didn't close my eyes and hum in place of a response. Veronica had me under a spell.

"Hello. I thought that was you." I looked up to see Professor Walker and another female colleague of mine whose name I couldn't recall.

"Liz?" Veronica questioned in a strained voice.

Shit! It was Elizabeth White from the Student Rights and Conduct Committee.

"You changed your hair. I told Vivian there was no way Nathaniel Brown was out with a student. But now that I can see you up close, I see I was wrong. I was just used to your old hairstyle," Liz said to Veronica with her hands crossed over her chest.

Professor Vivian Walker had no trace of a smile on her face as she

90

regarded me angrily. I knew a jealous and vindictive woman when I saw one. I'd better draft an email immediately or maybe call President Reed after dinner. Wait, I hadn't done anything wrong. Technically, it was a conflict of interest since my name was on Veronica's case, but I hadn't consulted on it in any way. I only knew the details of it because I looked it up out of curiosity. These women needed to mind their damn business.

"Uh, yeah, I cut it recently. Look—" Veronica started, but I wouldn't let her finish. These grown ass women were not about to intimidate her in front of me.

"Professor Walker, Elizabeth, Veronica and I are having a private, consensual dinner and we'd like to continue it. If there's something you'd like to ask me about school-related issues, I'd love to speak with you next week on campus. For now, this is my personal time." I was fair, but firm in my tone.

I'd taken a stance of admission to being out with a student and the belief there was no wrong in my actions. This shit could come to bite me in the ass, but I would not be intimidated, or allow Veronica to be intimidated, by two hating ass grown women. Veronica shifted next to me. Her eyes bounced between mine and the ladies'.

"I look forward to it," Professor Walker spoke for the first time. There was no flirtation in her voice or delight in her eyes. In my last encounter with Professor Walker, she was contorted inappropriately in front of me. She'd made it obvious her attraction to me, but now, she looked downright enraged I was out with someone other than her.

Shit! I knew this girl would get my ass into trouble the first time I found her number and called it. The reality was, I didn't give a shit, and none of it made me want to stop my pursuit of her; not her student status or her misconduct. Chantel V. Waters had a hold on me, and I had no fucking complaints about it.

A young waitress with the pose and striking features of an aspiring actress approached the table and asked if the other women would join us for dinner.

"They were just leaving," I said to officially dismiss them. Liz rolled her eyes at Veronica and Professor Walker glared at me as they stormed off. I wondered how long it would take before they reported me. If they did, I was prepared to double down for this girl. If anything, their disapproval made me want Veronica more.

"Can I get you started with drinks?" the waitress asked.

"Yes. A martini, extra dry," Veronica blurted in a distressed tone.

"Damn, OK. You got any Hennessy VSOP?" I added to Veronica's drink request.

"Yes, sir," the waitress said with a smile. "I'll be right back with those."

"So now you're really trying to get me in trouble. I know your young ass is not twenty-one."

"I'm a few months short. If you are only sort of in a power dynamic as it pertains to my student status, I'm only sort of underage."

I cleared my throat as irrational fantasies of Veronica opposite me in the courtroom flashed before my eyes. The banter between us riled me up, and there was nothing sexier than her defense against my underage line of questions. *What the hell is wrong with me? I need some ass!* I thought.

"Shit, OK." I was generally a laid-back type of person, but Veronica had me shook. I wouldn't let her see it, but on the inside, I screamed to take her from the restaurant to my place.

The speakers on the patio caught my attention. They'd played instrumentals and background noise until then. I heard the silky tone of Usher and his croon of "There Goes My Baby". I loved this song and, despite my better judgment, I had an unshakeable urge to hold Veronica close to my body.

I stood, and once I was on the opposite side of her, I extended my hand down toward her. Her breath caught as realization covered her bright features.

"Come dance with me." I didn't ask because I wanted her to know I needed her to oblige.

She stood and ran her hand across the back of her short, natural hair. Each time she did, it drew my attention to her neck. I fought fantasies of me behind her, sprinkling kisses down the area.

"This is not a real dance floor. Nobody else is dancing."

"Since when do you care what other people are doing?" I asked.

Veronica's face was sassy as she craned her neck up to meet my gaze.

I ignored it and pulled her small body close to me like I'd set out to. She smelled like candy. Not in an immature way, but in a slight body mist manner. I hadn't been accosted with a strong perfume like I did when I was around other women. Her scent required close proximity, and it felt like a reward versus an overzealous attempt to get anyone in a one-mile radius to smell her.

"What song is this?" she asked as she allowed me to guide her body slowly in place.

"Oh, hell naw." I couldn't believe her young ass didn't know this song. It was before my time, too, but I'd heard it.

"I mean, I know it's Usher. It's Usher, right?" Her nose crinkled up and her face was playful. I loved to see her this way. Though she was uncomfortable because I'd asked her to dance in public where there was no dance floor, the conversation she participated in was light-hearted. She didn't seem stressed at all; I wanted Veronica to stress less. I wanted it for me, too, especially after the video chat I'd had with Zanaé.

"Girl, this is a deal breaker." I stopped my movement, but she pressed her body closer.

"Are you sure about that?" Veronica's small breasts unintentionally rubbed against the area between my abs and chest. I resumed the dance to avoid the overtly sensual contact. We were in public, and I didn't want a fully hard dick.

"The song is called 'There Goes My Baby'," I said to deflect from my lustful feelings.

"I like it. *There goes my baby*," she sang. I'd closed my eyes momentarily as she sang, then hummed the melody of the words she didn't know. After a moment or so, my eyes sprang open.

"Shit. You can sing!"

"I do a little something." She winked up at me when she said it.

I wanted to ask her more about the voice that was as beautiful as it was seductive, but decided I didn't have to have all my questions answered right now. Instead, I chose to be in the moment and enjoy the time I had where I wasn't worried about work or my home life. Veronica was fire, but she was also the breath of fresh air I didn't know I needed.

We danced for another two songs when the waitress finally set our drinks on the table beside us. Veronica wiggled from my embrace and rubbed her hands through her short curls. She looked embarrassed.

"Your drinks have been ready for some time. I just didn't want to interrupt such an intimate moment."

"Thank you," I said appreciatively.

"I'll give you some time to look over your menu." The waitress hurried off like she'd caught us kissing.

The rest of dinner was a blur. I could barely focus. I found Veronica's mannerisms suggestive in every way. She took a bite of food and hummed appreciatively. She caught my moan in response to hers, and I was only slightly stilted. I cut the waitress off when she offered dessert because my treat was seated in a sundress beside me. I hoped like hell she would let me unwrap her.

I took care of the bill when the waitress brought the sable-colored restaurant bill folder. She'd barely placed it on the table before I slipped my card in it and handed it back. Veronica shifted beside me.

"You good?"

"Yep."

I wasn't convinced by her response, so I kept on. "Did you want dessert? I didn't mean to decide for you."

"No, Big Nate. I'm waiting for you to ask to come back to my place or invite me to yours." Her light eyes bore into mine and I felt like my dick moaned. She hadn't tiptoed around the issue, and it was by far, one of the most attractive things a woman could do, in my opinion.

"Well, shit. Let me get my card back and I will gladly take you home. I enjoy the view from my villa, and I'd like to share it with you."

When the waitress returned with my card, I signed the paper quickly and all but dragged Veronica out front to retrieve my car from the valet. She was distant again. I wondered if this was a pattern of hers, or if I'd come on too strong. I wanted her, and I'd been vocal about it. Maybe she hadn't planned to end up in bed with me as soon as I suggested it.

I pulled her body toward me as we waited for my car, and she melted into me without resistance. The night air was chilly for Veronica, but I was unbothered by it.

"How cold is it where you're from?" she asked with her eyes focused on the street in front of us.

"I'm from Ohio. You say it like I'm from another planet."

"It may as well be." This time, she did crane her neck up to meet my gaze. She was so fine from this angle. Without a second thought, I leaned down and planted an unhurried kiss on her full lips. She kissed me back and turned her body to fully face me.

Veronica leaned up and wrapped her thin arms around my neck and it took everything I had not to lift her and wrap her legs around my waist. I wanted to feel more of her right fucking now, but I knew this wasn't the place. I settled for a taste of her tongue, which caressed mine seductively.

I groaned when the valet chose that particular moment to pull up alongside us with my car. When I opened my eyes, hers remained closed. I took the opportunity to plant a quick kiss on her freckles. I'd wanted to kiss them since the first time I saw her on campus. *Shit. Again, what the hell am I doing?*

I'd seen Professor Walker and Elizabeth White while at this very restaurant with an ENEP student. It should have been enough to shake me out of whatever dream state I was in. This would not end well, and yet, I had no intention of slowing down. If Veronica kept her mouth and her body available to me, I would partake, consequences be damned. I knew I should head home to call or draft an email to Professor Reed, but the look on Veronica's face let me know I was about to get lucky. There was no way I would turn her down.

The car ride to my house was serene. The sun had set, but the glimpses of the ocean and the sound of the waves was plenty for our ears to take in. Veronica hummed and the vibration of her voice hit me right between my legs. I recognized the song; it was the Usher track again. It must have made an impression on her, and it put a huge smile on my face.

"Siri, play 'There Goes My Baby'." She regarded me briefly with a sensual smirk. *Damn, she's fine!* My dick jumped and I cleared my throat.

The familiar words of the song played softly as Veronica sang along. As I listened to her harp-like rasps, I felt like I could feel the music in my body. I cleared my throat again as she rested her hand on my thigh. *I'm*

95

going to crash if she doesn't remove her hand. Fuck, I'm definitely killing us if she moves it at all.

She stroked my thigh as Usher crooned. Veronica switched the words and belted, *"Ooh, boy, look at you"*. I blushed and felt like a damn groupie in her presence.

This girl could have a motive when it came to me. I was fully aware she could be using me for an end goal, by way of her seductive powers, yet I couldn't seem to make myself give a damn. Veronica felt me shift underneath her touch and it was the ammunition she needed to continue to drive me wild.

Her hand inched further up my thigh until it reached my dick. I glanced over at her, and her expression made it clear she wouldn't stop until I insisted she do so. I wasn't convinced she'd stop then.

"You like that, professor?"

"Mmhm." I gritted my teeth. I didn't really want her to stop, but I also didn't want to wreck.

Her tiny hands found my belt buckle and she undid it with minimal effort. I irrationally wondered how many times she'd done something like this. I didn't have much time to stew in unwarranted jealousy because, the next thing I knew, her hands had made their way into my pants and my boxer briefs.

"Mmhm!" I moaned again. Her hands felt so damn good on me. If I had second thoughts about Veronica, I needed to stop this now.

I heard her seatbelt click and my heart dropped the same time the car swerved. *She can't be about to do what I think she's about to do.* Veronica leaned her body over and angled her head between my legs. I wanted this shit more than my last breath, but I wasn't confident I could maintain focus on the road if she did.

She put her hot mouth on the tip of my dick, and I swerved again.

"Look, baby, you gotta sit back and wait 'til I pull over."

She sat back and crossed her arms across her chest in a full-on pout. The shit was so cute; it relieved the sexual tension that built up with her last kiss.

"Fine. Are we almost here?" Veronica rolled her eyes and huffed as if maybe I wasn't the only one pent up.

"Yeah, baby. We're almost here."

. . .

I PULLED INTO MY NEIGHBORHOOD, and Veronica's demeanor shifted once again. My mind told me she was an unpredictable, unstable girl I needed to steer clear of. But my heart wouldn't accept it. She'd just put her pretty face between my legs, and now she felt a million miles away. *Am I supposed to ask her what's up? Or assume she didn't actually want to fuck me, just toy with me?*

"Did I say something stupid?" I asked as I scratched the back of my head.

"I can't be here."

I'd pulled into my driveway and stilled at her words. Maybe she did get a kick out of seeing me riled up. The mixed signals had me confused as hell. *She was into me, right? So what the hell changed?*

"This is where I filmed them. Nina lives here," she said quietly. "I can't be here," she repeated.

Twelve

VERONICA

"SHIT." Nate scratched the back of his head like he always did when he was in deep thought. As uncomfortable as I was to be near the scene of the crime, so to speak, his mannerisms put me at ease. *He is so damn cute when he's frazzled*, I thought.

"I can't be here," I repeated for the third time. I'd made progress with Dr. DeLucchi and my requirements from the dean. The last thing I wanted to do was violate the terms of my probation with school. If nothing else, I was determined to graduate. *What would happen if Rashad and Nina saw me here?* She'd be well within her rights to call the police or report me to ENEP.

"Where does she live?"

"She lives here, Nate. I just told you I can't be here like seventy times," I exaggerated.

"I heard your sassy ass. But where? The units on my side are letter P. 'P' like please stop being difficult and tell me where she lives so I can decide whether we can be here."

I thought for a long time. My brain finally focused on his question, because part of me liked it when Big Nate begged. The night I made the video, I parked and walked to her villa. When I saw her back out of her driveway, I noticed a big letter 'D' on the front of her mailbox.

"It was D. 'D' like I enjoyed the taste of your D in my mouth." He didn't respond. Instead, he hopped out of his car and was on my side in a matter of seconds. He undid my seatbelt and lifted me so my ass sat comfortably on his left arm. I instinctively wrapped my arms around his neck.

He closed my car door and only returned me to my feet to unlock the front door to his home, like it was perfectly normal for him to handle me this way. A small yelp escaped my lips when he did.

"What about Nina?"

He didn't move his eyes from the door when he responded, "I've run this entire beachfront at least twice and D units are almost a mile from here."

I was gently tugged inside before I could comment.

The inside of Nate's villa made me feel like I'd crossed over into another universe. I expected it to feel stuffy because he was an academic. I'd misread him. Though there was no TV in the sitting area, the space felt warm and inviting. I was comfortable in his home and felt like I could relax here. It smelled like him, but also like he kept it clean.

There was a heavy bag near the patio door; I imagined how hot he looked as he beat the shit out of it. Nate was a controlled man, but everyone needed an outlet. There was an expensive chess board set up with all the pieces meticulously arranged. Only, instead of standard white and black pieces, Nate's were gray and clear.

I could appreciate what must have been his office in a room to the right. I couldn't see all the area, but I did see a distressed brown leather sofa. It was the most lawyer aspect of his home.

"Come here."

Nate sat on the enormous navy-blue sectional that contrasted beautifully against his light-colored walls and light stained hardwood floors. The throw pillows and blanket were cream colored, and I had to shake a wave of jealousy. Had a woman helped him decorate?

"I said come here, Chantel." He'd added bass in his voice, and I couldn't remember the last time I wanted to comply with a man's command.

I walked over to him as his watchful gaze escorted me over. When I was finally within his reach, he pulled me onto his lap. He used his large, rough hands and rubbed my neck and the exposed skin on my back. I was unashamed of the moan that escaped my lips. I'd wanted Big Nate's hands on me since we were at dinner.

I couldn't wait any longer. I turned my head and his lips quickly found mine. I relished the taste of Hennessy on his tongue when we kissed. My pulse quickened as his tongue explored the inside of my mouth. His hands found the inside of my flimsy dress and my nipples stood against the contact with his fingers.

He pulled them as he continued to make out with me. His thumb worked my nipple as his head lowered to the breast closest to him. I shifted so I faced him in his lap to give him full access. I felt my insides tighten as he licked one nipple and fondled the other. *Double damn!* I was about to cum, and he wasn't even inside me.

I threw my head back and let wave after wave crash inside of my center. My legs shook and I was a little embarrassed I'd orgasmed so quickly. I looked up to see a smirk on his beautiful, bronzed face.

"I wanna feel you inside of me, Nate."

He said nothing, just shifted me off his lap and led me toward his bedroom. The view outside took my breath and I momentarily forgot how badly I wanted the D. The sky was brightly lit by a full moon, impeded only slightly by a few clouds. The water was dark, but the waves were white where they met the beach's edge.

Nate's California King was propped up on a platform. It was positioned so it faced the sliding patio door with the view that had me in a trance. When I saw the bed, I dropped my sundress. I only wore a thin, black thong underneath. Nate took in a quick breath, like he was in pain when his eyes connected with my body.

I walked over to him, undid the button on his suit jacket, and removed it from his broad shoulders.

"You sure about this, Chantel?"

"You playing, right?"

"No, I'm serious. Once I enter you, things will never be the same. I'm not one of these ENEP boys. If we do this, you belong to me."

"Do I look like I'm going anywhere?" I huffed. He could have access to every part of me. I needed to feel his dick, and I needed to feel it now.

"I'm serious. I don't fuck to be fucking. I can give you as many orgasms as you want, but if I go inside of you, I expect to be the only one who gets that privilege. I'm kind of springing this on you and I want to make sure you're not just agreeing because I'm putting you on the spot."

I smiled at him thoughtfully. "You're right. I'm not used to dating anyone like you. I tease you about bagging a professor, but I genuinely like you. I want you to fuck me until I scream and I couldn't imagine it happening only once."

"I'm not gonna share you. Your situation or the man you were dealing with—." He was tight and his jaw was clenched when he started his sentence. I never thought I'd go for a territorial man, but my thong was drenched.

"I told you I wasn't dealing with anyone else. My life was a mess until recently. Are you applying for the position of my man?"

"Something like that. I'm just not into sharing. Of course, we gotta get to know each other better, but I'm not willing to do that while you entertain other men. Like I said before, once I enter you, it won't be the same."

"Nate, if you don't give me your fucking dick already." This man was going to torture me to death with his talking ass.

He leaned down and kissed me on my neck.

"Let's pray first?" he said in a baritone voice.

"What?" I asked breathily.

"I wanna pray with you first."

"Nate, I say 'fuck' and 'damn' too much for that," I said, uncomfortable with a discussion about the Lord at a time such as this.

"Me too, baby. But Black Jesus knows my heart." He grabbed my hands, dropped his head, and closed his eyes. He was as serious as a heart attack. I moaned and shifted impatiently. I would do anything to feel the print between his legs, so I dropped my heathen head and closed my eyes.

"Black Jesus, thank you for bringing Veronica into my life. Remove anything that would hinder our ability to reach our highest possible level of sexual satisfaction. May we both be in tune with our bodies and spirits. Let this act be an opportunity to connect with you and our highest selves.

"Black Jesus, let whatever is manifested between us tonight yield more goodness and freedom. Remove anything that would prevent Chantel from being comfortable in her skin or present in her body with me. Let it be the best we've ever had.

"Thank you for sex as an act of expression and liberation. Thank you for consent, for safety, and for this meal I'm about to receive, Amen." He smirked down at me when he mentioned the meal part and I briefly wondered if I might be in over my head.

MY FACE WAS SHOVED into his mattress as he pounded into me. The contact felt as satisfying as it did painful.

"The hell you doin' with a pussy this good?"

I couldn't respond, but I twerked my ass to intensify the pleasure for us both. I had gotten Nate so hot and bothered when I put my mouth on him during the drive, he ravaged me the moment we said amen and he'd put a condom on.

The prayer hadn't been super religious at all. He asked for anything that could possibly hinder our highest pleasure to be removed. Nate called in sensuality between us as a form of prayer and connection with our highest selves. I felt my insides melt and my mind orgasm as he spoke over us.

Once again, I'd misjudged him. I thought for sure he'd be the slow grind, make love type of man, but I couldn't have been more off base. Nate punished my pussy like I deserved it for making him wait too long. I thought I was the impatient one, but apparently, he'd been cool on the outside and riled up on the inside.

He'd yanked my thong down, lifted me, and entered me when I wrapped my legs around him; I came on contact. He fucked me against the wall until I got a rug burn on my back. He noticed when I winced and promptly moved me to the bed where my head was currently smashed into the mattress. I was on the verge of orgasm number three. His stamina was unmatched, and I feared I'd fall in love with him based solely on how he put in work.

He stilled. When I lifted my gaze to see what happened, his brows were knitted together.

"What's wrong?"

"Did you know your pussy was this good?"

I smirked. *What the hell was I supposed to say? Didn't every girl think they had the best pussy?*

He backed away from me and I whined my disapproval.

"I need you to ride me."

I hopped up so quickly, I almost fell trying to obey. I hustled to the edge of the bed where he sat and attempted to mount him, but he stopped me.

"Face the window and watch the ocean with me, baby."

I'll be damned if I didn't cum as I stood beside him. My legs shook at his gruff tone and the look in his eyes. His lids were lowered like he was inebriated. When he realized I'd had my third orgasm, he smirked and told me to get ready for number four.

I sat on his lap and faced away from him. He started the slow grind I thought he'd be on from the beginning. He held one hand against my neck and pushed inside of me. He used the other hand to play between my legs. I maneuvered myself on my tiptoes and felt him shift from upright to a leaned back position.

He moved his hand to grab my short hair while the other clutched my waist as he continued deep, slow strokes.

"You got one more for me, baby?"

I moaned in place of a response. There was no way I could orgasm again without literally blacking out.

"Fuck that, baby. I need to hear you. If you want this professor to bring your grade up, then you better cum one last time and catch this nut."

My legs shook. I was balanced on my toes and my thighs ached. None of that stopped the tension and build of electricity once again. "I'm about to cum, professor."

"Good, because I'm about to cum with you."

THE NEXT MORNING, my legs felt numb. I had no clue what time it was. Nate reached for me throughout the night, and I honestly lost count of how many times we had sex. It was the best I'd ever had. I probably wouldn't admit it to him right away, though.

I slid from under Nate's heavy arm and ambled to the bathroom. His bathroom was bright, and I squinted my eyes in frustration that they were open. After I did my business and washed my hands, I returned to his bedroom to find the most breathtaking sunrise.

"Come here."

I quickly did as I was told. I climbed onto Nate's bed and laid on my stomach. I wasn't ready for another round but was too tired to use words. Nate inched his way down to my waist and laid his head on my bare ass cheeks.

"Damn, your ass is soft."

I giggled. I was small and didn't receive many compliments on my backside. We lay in that position for another thirty minutes or so before I felt him shake me awake.

"Veronica." I sat up, dazed.

"I need more sleep." I looked over at his bedside clock and saw it was eight a.m.

"Take a run with me."

I groaned and pulled the covers over my head. The next thing I knew, Nate pulled them away. The chill against my naked skin jarred me awake. I sat and threw him a steely gaze.

"What the fuck?" I liked Nate, but I wasn't up for games. I was not a morning person.

"Damn, sassy ass. You look like you're about to slap the shit out of me. I'm going for a run, and I want you to come with me," he said sincerely.

I rolled my eyes and laid back down with my ass to him. He chuckled and pulled my legs to the edge of the bed. I jumped up and into his face, as far as I could with the height difference.

"What the hell is your problem? It's too early for this."

He peered down at me, and my anger melted. "Please."

I crossed my arms over my chest and a smile crept across my face. "I don't have any clothes. I came over in my dress and heels."

"What size do you wear?"

"What?"

"What size shoe fits those little doll feet?"

"Nate..." I whined.

"You can sleep while I go buy your clothes."

"Do you want me to lose weight or something?" My voice was laced with an attitude. It was too damn early for this.

"No. But it will make you feel better, trust me."

NATE WENT OVERBOARD with the clothes. Not only did he buy me three workout outfits and two pairs of shoes, but he also bought me a yellow maxi dress so I wouldn't have to do a walk of shame as he so eloquently put it. It was sweet, and the clothes were cute.

He was also right about the run. After he returned with workout gear for me and promised I wouldn't run into Nina, we ran on the beach. I didn't hate it as much as I thought. I was in decent shape, but I did need to stop a few times. He was patient with me and seemed to genuinely enjoy my company.

We finished our run, and Nate made breakfast while I showered. I liked to be the one on the receiving end of the spoiling for once. Nate's food was great. During breakfast, I made fun of him because he didn't have a TV and called him an old man for the thousandth time. He said I wasn't cultured and challenged me to a game of chess.

I beat the professor and I beat him quickly. I shared with him how my stepdad played chess with me because he was an old man, too. Nate wasn't a complete sore loser, but he did bite me on the ass when I taunted him. I felt energized, despite the beating he put on me the night before. The run and the food motivated me to face my errands and test prep for the weekend.

Nathaniel Brown walked hand in hand with me to his car. He kissed me goodbye before he pulled out of the driveway to take me back to my place. It was the sweetest and most unexpected date I'd ever had. I hoped he wouldn't get in trouble for our night together. I'd never forgive myself if he did.

Thirteen

NATE

I COULDN'T GET Veronica off my mind after I dropped her off. I tried my best not to text or call her, but only made it a day and a half before I did.

Me: *You're on your way to an A in my course*

Chantel Veronica MINE: *You're so nasty*

Me: *Do you want me to stop?*

Chantel Veronica MINE: *Hell no. But seriously, are you going to get in trouble for... you know?*

Me: *For what?*

Chantel Veronica MINE: *Don't play with me*

Me: *Say it*

Chantel Veronica MINE: *For fucking my brains out*

Me: *Speaking of brains*

Chantel Veronica MINE: *Omg, you're so nasty*

Me: *And you like it. You never finished... you know.*

Chantel Veronica MINE: *I don't know. Say it.* *Purple devil emoji

Me: *Shit. Can I see you this week?*

Chantel Veronica MINE: *So I can finish what I started in your car*

I'd started to choke because this girl was so damn nasty.

Chantel Veronica MINE: *Are you over there choking old man?*

Me: *Shit!*
Chantel Veronica MINE: *LOL. Get back to work, professor. I have a test in an hour. Wish me luck.*
Me: *Good lick. I mean, good luck Chantel*
Chantel Veronica MINE: *Lip bite emoji

I WAS POSTED outside of my office at ENEP because I was bored and done with class for the day. I wanted Veronica back in my bed, but I needed to clear the air with President Reed before Professor Walker could. My phone rang in my hand and startled the shit out of me. It was an unknown number, and I wondered if it was someone from Zanaé's team.

"Nathaniel Brown," Anton sang.

"Hey, Anton, what's up?"

I'd won Anton over after I connected him with my mentor. Turns out, the couple uploaded the security guard incident with Zanaé to social media, but each platform removed the video. Anton was sent a copy, so both my mentor and I saw it. How she described it paled in comparison to the footage. My stomach churned at the thought of her attack.

Since my mentor and his team had gotten onboard, the FéTim issued an official statement to apologize to Zanaé. It was a bullshit attempt to do damage control and only pissed everyone off further. The guard was terminated, and the hotel settled with Zanaé for an undisclosed amount of money.

In the end, she wanted to move forward and didn't feel she could heal if things were dragged out in court. She was rich before, but if I knew my mentor, Zanaé would collect checks from the FéTim until she left this earth and possibly after.

"Nothing much. We're in the area and someone wants to thank you in person." I heard his smile through the phone. He wasn't completely impatient with me anymore, but he still made fun of how off balance I was in Zanaé's presence.

I cleared my throat. "Shit, OK."

"Turn around, boy scout."

I turned around and saw an entourage headed in my direction. A small group of students followed as Zanaé's team approached. I couldn't see her in the crowd, but she was tiny and I was sure she was securely surrounded. I stood there like an idiot. *Am I supposed to wait here or walk up to her?* Goliath and Anton gave me a nod, so I met them halfway.

Zanaé emerged from the circle of people, and a gang of cameras appeared.

"Damn, you good?" I asked as I scratched the back of my head.

"It comes with the job, Nate," Zanaé said with the sultry voice I'd gotten somewhat used to.

"Thank you again, man," Rod, Zanaé's man, said as he grabbed my hand and shook it appreciatively. "I'm serious, thank you for all you and your mentor did for my girl."

"Absolutely, bro. I'd want someone to do the same for my lady." My mind drifted to thoughts of Veronica. She wasn't the victim; she'd been the accused, and yet, I'd step in for her at the drop of a hat. I laid Rashad out and I'd do it again, dammit.

"Lady?" Zanaé gazed up at me. She was a naturally charismatic person. I guess it was a hazard of the job. She reached her tiny hand up and grabbed my facial hair. "Oh my gosh. You have a girlfriend?" she asked with a twinkle in her eye.

"Baby, don't go meddling in this man's business," her guy added as he picked up his phone and sidestepped the crowd. He gave me a nod as he tended to his call.

"Is she cute?"

Anton snickered. "Knowing him, it's probably a coworker."

I stiffened. *Why the hell was I always on trial with them?*

He gasped. "It's not a coworker. It's a student."

Zanaé and Anton locked eyes and laughed as if I were an episode of *Love & Hip Hop.*

"I mean, yeah, but she's not in my class or anything." I scratched the back of my head as the two of them erupted in laughter.

Zanaé hugged me as she said, "I just love this guy. You can't be all good, Nate. Otherwise, I'd worry about you."

"I thought he was sleeping with the assistant," Anton said and redirected his attention to his phone.

I felt eyes on me. I looked around and there was a larger crowd gathered to catch a glimpse at Zanaé. I saw Professor Walker first, but she was always mad these days. Then my gaze connected with the honey-colored eyes of Chantel Veronica, and she was... pissed. Zanaé still had me in an embrace, but I didn't want Zanaé. I mean, not for real.

"My girl is here," I told them.

"Cool. I wanna meet her," Zanaé said.

"Really? She can sing, too. So, she's gotta be a fan."

"Boy Scout, don't undo all the cool you built trying to put a student you're sleeping with on," Anton huffed with fake annoyance.

"No, it's nothing like that. She'd probably kill me if she knew I said she can sing. She's one of those closeted creatives."

"Ohhhh," they sang together as if what I'd said made perfect sense to the two of them.

As we made our way closer, and the students parted, I saw Veronica's demeanor shift from pissed to enraged. She looked like she would bite my head off. *Is she really tripping over Zanaé?* It was obvious this girl was out of my league. And if there was something going on between us, I wouldn't have fucked Veronica until her legs were numb and claimed her the way I did less than forty-eight hours ago.

She had a thick, sexy girl beside her with a curly afro who had her phone out and spoke loudly. I wondered if she was one of her sorority sisters. Veronica hadn't blinked, but her friend yelled something about some kid named Tony who couldn't reach Veronica, so he'd been blowing her up.

Was he the man she was entertaining before me? Was she still fucking him? Anton's super observant ass saw the same scene unfold as I did. "Aw, shit," he said when he saw Veronica's face. "I don't think Boy Scout's girl is down for an introduction today."

"Veronica," I called out over the crowd of people screaming for Zanaé. She didn't respond, just stared at me.

I halted my steps as she took the phone from her friend and spoke to whoever couldn't get ahold of her.

"The fuck?" I said with my brows jumbled across my forehead.

· · ·

ZANAÉ WAS KIND ENOUGH to speak to students and sign a few autographs. She asked me to stay so the team could take me out for lunch and, of course, I agreed. Goliath broke up the crowd once Zanaé had enough, and they pulled me into the entourage with them. We were met with a stretch black limo in the employee parking lot of ENEP's campus.

I wanted to connect with the conversation that happened around me, but I couldn't shake my disappointment in Veronica. *What the hell kind of games was she on? And who the hell did she take a phone call from? Didn't she know that was my pussy?* But more importantly, I wouldn't be disrespected. What she did was not only disrespectful, but it was also childish as hell. If she had any questions, she should use her words and ask me directly.

"So, Naé said your girl was in the crowd?" Rod asked.

"Yeah, man, but she was on some other stuff." I scratched the back of my head because I was kind of embarrassed.

"I get it," he said matter-of-factly.

"You get what?" She'd acted like a child, and I was too damn old for this kind of shit.

"You know how many people grab my lady by her lower back or lean in for a kiss when they know the paparazzi are around?" I knew exactly what he meant. And because she hadn't gone public with their relationship, I was sure the media crafted all types of imaginary liaisons for Zanaé. "I almost lost her, so I didn't have the luxury of unwarranted jealousy. Naé says your girl is a student?"

Anton and Goliath laughed. I was too pissed to be offended, so I nodded my response.

"I ask because it means she's young. If you put something down on her and then she sees you in an embrace with Naé, that's damning, bro."

"But she could've asked me instead of jumping to conclusions," I said through gritted teeth.

"Exactly," Zanaé chimed in. "I knew I liked you!"

"You're both Libras," Anton said, as he rolled his eyes and returned to his phone. This man stayed conducting business, no matter where he was.

"But I had to learn to see things from Rod's perspective. I think you should do the same, boy scout," Zanaé added.

"Huh?"

"Imagine if your girl was with a mega famous actor, or a guy from a group who got panties thrown at him regularly, and you saw him with his hands on her like mine were on you."

My jaw clenched. Zanaé had a point. I'd be pissed if Veronica were hugged up with anyone other than me. The difference between Veronica and me was, I'd tell her the shit was unacceptable instead of choosing another woman to entertain. If she was on the games, it was going to be a hard pass for me. I told her Friday night I wouldn't share. *Did she think that only applied to her? If I didn't want her with other men while we figured out what we were, why would she think I'd turn around and entertain other women?*

It was obvious this girl didn't trust or respect me, and I didn't have the brain capacity for that shit.

DRINKS WITH ZANAÉ, her man, and her team was lit. I was able to somewhat enjoy myself, despite my annoyance with Veronica. Goliath asked for Yazmin, my assistant from Ohio's, phone number. I gave him a hard time about it, but eventually agreed to text her his info. I'd effectively gelled with everyone in the group, including Zanaé's man.

They'd gotten the celebrity treatment from the time we arrived at the lounge until we'd left. They returned me to campus where my car was parked and promised we would get together when Zanaé had more time.

My head throbbed as I walked to my car from where they'd dropped me off. I had a few drinks and I kept wondering if she had her mouth on another man to make me crazy. My phone vibrated in my pants. When I pulled it out, I saw it was Veronica. I declined her call. I needed space to process this shit. I decided I'd catch a movie and maybe a little space would help me figure out my next move.

I could tolerate a lot. I hadn't judged Veronica for her social misconduct or her young age. I poked fun at her, but it was all good natured.

What I wouldn't tolerate was a woman who jumped to conclusions and couldn't give me the benefit of the doubt.

As I exited the ENEP employee parking, I prayed the movie theater would have a martial arts film to provide the escape I desperately needed.

Fourteen

VERONICA

I FELT like things had fallen into place in my life for the first time. I was confident I'd just passed my test. I was in good standing with my probationary requirements, and I had a man with a big dick and a pure heart interested in me. I had a goofy smile on my face as I left the building next to the library where my class was held.

"Damn, V, who puttin' in that kinda work to have you all smiles and giggles?" Lisa asked as she walked over to meet me.

"You don't know him. And I'll cut you if you even think about sleeping with him."

"Woooooow! It must have been good for you to get all tight."

"It was." I left the conversation there. I still wasn't sure if Nate could get in trouble because of our arrangement, whatever it was. And Lisa couldn't keep a secret any better than she could keep her damn legs closed.

"Bitch! Somebody just tweeted Zanaé's on campus. Come on."

I sang her music when I cleaned my apartment. I oddly felt like I knew her on a spiritual level. She also made bad bitch anthems I would swear were penned just for a former bad girl like myself.

We were a few steps from where Lisa saw the tweet when we saw a large group of students. I had an even bigger cheesy grin on my face as we made our way through the crowd to get a closer look. That was when I saw Nate, my fucking Nate, in a cozy embrace with Zanaé. *The fuck? Had he fucked her? Was she better than me? Did he pray with that bitch?*

"V, Tony is blowing my phone up, looking for you. Please talk to this man," Lisa said loudly.

I didn't give a shit what Tony had to say. Lisa said he'd called her nonstop for the past week or so because she posted a picture of us on her social media. Apparently, he liked my new hair but was aware I'd blocked him.

I couldn't believe my eyes. My fucking man was hugged up with a got damn pop star icon. I felt like fire built in my belly and steam shot from my ears like they did on the cartoons. Nate saw me and seemed confused by my expression.

I accepted Tony's call because I didn't know what else to do. I'd been played the moment I allowed myself to open up. *I knew it! Look where this good girl shit got me.* When I took the phone from Lisa, the professor flinched. I couldn't care less. If he wanted to see a savage, here I was.

I TALKED to Tony for about five minutes before I realized I'd made a mistake. He didn't care about me as a person. He wanted to link up regardless of what I'd been up to. It felt... wrong. I said goodbye to Lisa for the day and decided to return to my apartment from campus. I had one class left, but I knew I wouldn't be able to concentrate, so I opted to skip it.

On the drive home, I contemplated popping up on Nate. He had the nerve to pray over the pussy, then let that bitch have her hands around his neck. The smile on her face matched the one I had over the weekend.

I was so uncomfortable because I could hear Dr. DeLucchi's annoying voice in my head. She taught me triggers would happen. The goal wasn't to avoid them, but to choose a different response when they came. *Fuck!*

"Siri, call Sadé."

"Hey, girl, hey!" Sade answered the call after only two rings.

That was when the tears fell. *It's OK to cry, Veronica!* My new thoughts sounded foreign and made me want to cry more. Only now, my tears felt loving and supportive. I couldn't wild out like Bad Bitch V if I wanted to.

"Talk to me, friend. What's going on?" Sadé's voice was gentle and felt like a much-needed warm embrace.

"There's a new guy. I really like him. I opened up to him and we took things to the next level this weekend."

Sade hummed her acknowledgement.

"He asked me to pray before we had sex, then today, I saw him hugged up with Zanaé."

"The hell? I mean... OK. He asked you to pray before you had sex?"

"Yes. It was the best I've ever had."

"I bet. I ain't never had a man pray before his meal."

As unhinged as I felt, her words made me laugh. We shared moments of healing giggles, and it gave me time to gather myself so I could continue the short drive to my apartment. I decided against the drive to Nate's villa.

"OK, and this man knows Zanaé the singer?" Sadé was so confused. I knew it must've sounded like I'd lost my mind.

"He's a lawyer. He probably knows lots of famous and powerful people."

"Shit! OK, girl." We shared more laughter until she continued. "What did he say when you asked him about it?"

"I didn't have a chance. I was so jealous, I took a call from someone I used to mess around with. He heard my sorority sister tell me the call was from Tony, so I entertained him to make Nate, the lawyer, jealous. I don't know what to do.

"I know what I did was childish, and a big part of me wants to ride over to his house to make sure she isn't there."

"I'm proud of you!" was Sadé's response.

"The hell? Did you hear what I just said? I took a call from someone to make Nate jealous. I didn't give him the benefit of the doubt, and I want to stalk his house in case he's there with Zanaé."

"I heard you. Let me ask you this. Before counseling, would you have called someone to talk?"

Silence stretched between us. I hadn't considered how much I had grown. She was right. A few short months ago, the old V would have walked up to Nate and slapped the shit out of him. I probably would have looked for his car to vandalize it without a second thought.

"No. Not Bad Girl V." I was able to find humor, despite the pain of the situation. I was officially on the road to recovery.

I HAD to be up early Tuesday morning for community service with the at-risk girls. So far, each meeting was filled with paperwork and trainings. Today would be the first time I would actually interact with the girls. To say I was nervous was an understatement. Teenage girls could be ruthless. I was one of the worst when I was their age.

I called Nate after my talk with Sadé last night to ask him if there was anything between him and Zanaé, but he sent me to voicemail. I couldn't blame him. I hadn't known him long, but I knew he had a low tolerance for disrespect. I thought about what I'd do if they had history on my thirty-minute drive to the group home. *What would I do if he didn't want to see me anymore? Whatever happens, I'll be here for you. We can do hard things.*

I'd initially scoffed at the mantras Dr. DeLucchi assigned me when we started our sessions, but my self-talk had improved drastically. I felt like I could focus on my life better without constant internal abuse. If Nate needed space, I'd give it to him and take care of myself like my good friend Sadé suggested I do.

THE GROUP HOME had a cabin style exterior. It looked like the girls were at a year-long camping trip instead of a preventative home before juvenile detention. I'd seen them in passing but hadn't met with them. The counselors were confident I had the exact background of someone these girls could connect with.

They only had two requirements for me: I was under no circumstances to put my hands on them and my consistency with them was mandatory. One late arrival and/or one no show would result in my removal from the site. I took those requirements seriously because I needed this community service to graduate.

Tuesday was designated as recreational time for the teens. I was to monitor them in the studio area of cabin B. I sat in a chair in the back of the room with a book. Five girls dressed in similar sweatpants and t-shirts filtered into the space. The variations of their attire reflected each of their personal styles.

One wore her sweatshirt tied around her waist while another knotted her t-shirt at her hip. They were adorable, but appeared as though they'd been forced to grow up too soon.

"Ugh. Another college student who will last a good three weeks," one of the brown-skinned, baby faced girls bit out.

"Facts. She look stuck up, too," another one responded. They spoke about me as if I weren't a few feet away from them. But if this was what they considered hardcore, I could do this all day.

After they set up their Bluetooth speaker, they blasted a Zanaé song. My throat went dry as my mind drifted to Nate. I wasn't supposed to use my phone, but I slipped it from my bag and sent him a quick text.

Me: *Professor, can we talk?*

I kept my phone in my hand long enough to see the bubbles appear and disappear. I rolled my eyes and returned my phone to my bag.

Two of them attempted the dance I'd memorized the first time I saw the music video for the track. It was a mostly innocent dance with undertones of sensuality. Zanaé did the dance on a football field with four of her other friends. The girls struggled with the flips and transitions.

I could help with this if they'd let me.

"You need to drop before the beat," I said from my seat. My arms were still crossed as I thought of how I may have blown things with Nate. Or he may have blown things with me if he had the balls to see Zanaé at the same time he was seeing me.

"What?" the loudest girl said with an attitude. I think her name was Crystal.

"I know her old butt can't do any better." Her friend high-fived her.

I stood and removed my Beta Delta Delta jacket.

"Start it from the chorus," I told Crystal. I think she only did it because she thought I'd make a fool of myself.

As the song picked up, I swirled my body and dropped before the beat. It was a quick drop split that looked more complicated than it was. They just needed better timing. I lifted from the ground and was promptly met with squeals, claps, and giggles.

The girls' hard exterior melted as they realized I had more to offer than they originally assumed. I used the rest of the hour to teach the girls Zanaé's entire dance. They left the session, bragging about how they would go viral on social media with their new moves.

I finished my community service with a new sense of purpose. I had something to offer, and it felt damn good!

Fifteen

NATE

I STILL HADN'T SPOKEN to Veronica since the Zanaé debacle. The worst part was, I missed her. I craved her sassy, sexy energy. I wanted to be inside of her again and punish her body for putting me through this shit. I'd run the villa twice because I was pissed she wasn't on the damn run with me.

Maybe Zanaé was right. Maybe I needed to give her the benefit of the doubt around her unsubstantial jealousy. What I couldn't get over was why she accepted the call from whoever the fuck Tony was. After my run, I did the heavy bag for almost an hour until my alarm reminded me my baby sister would fly in soon. I needed to shower and get dressed so I could pick her up. Time with Talley would definitely lift my spirits.

"NATE THE GREAT!" Talley hugged me like it'd been years since we were in the same space. I lifted her and spun her around because I missed her more than I realized.

"Where are your clothes?" I asked with my face twisted up. NaTalley was a beautiful girl, but I wasn't used to grown-up Talley. She showed parts of her body I'd rather nobody see, including me.

"I'm dressed like a nun compared to these fifty feet tall model chicks." Her face sparkled with innocence, and I remembered how my mom warned me to look out for her.

"I'm not their brother, I'm yours. You got your thighs all on display and your short haircut trimmed up. Please don't make me break somebody's neck."

I quickly helped her into my car, so she was safely tucked behind my tinted windows, away from the interested glances of random men. Then I put her bags in the trunk of my car so we could head to my place.

Talley filled me in on everything I'd missed since I'd been gone while I drove her from the airport into town. She said Dad was starting to misplace things more often, so she'd taught him about brain teasers. I was grateful she was close to them now that I'd relocated, but the more time I spent in California, the less the move felt temporary. I longed for the three of them all to move here with me.

"I texted Demetrius to tell him I was here. He stopped texting when I asked him to introduce me to some of his teammates." She laughed, but I knew it probably had D out of his mind. "I'll just text his wifey."

"Anyway, let's stop at my place first so we can drop off your things, then we'll take you to campus."

We pulled up and I thought I was hallucinating until Talley took the words out of my mouth. "Who is this? You expecting company?"

"Uh." I scratched the back of my head. This could go left real quick. Veronica was seated on the steps that led to my front door. I had no idea how long she'd been there, or what she was up to.

"She's cute, Nate," Talley said as she pushed my head from the passenger seat. "And young. She looks like she's my age."

Talley and I exited the car as Veronica stood. She had on a pair of booty shorts similar to the ones my little sister wore. Only, Veronica's thin frame looked edible beneath her jean cut-offs. *Shit. I can't do this shit right now.*

"Hi. I'm NaTalley," Talley said as she held her hand out toward Veronica. Veronica flinched as if she assumed Talley was yet another love interest. This girl still didn't have enough respect to ask me instead of jumping to conclusions.

"Hi. Veronica," she said, deflated as she accepted Talley's hand. "I see you have company. I'm gonna head out," she threw in my general direction. She couldn't even look me in the eye.

Fuck! She walked past me, and my body tightened. I missed her, I was sexually frustrated, but most importantly, I needed her to be more mature than it seemed she was capable of. *Fuck!*

Sixteen

VERONICA

"YOU'RE MAKING TREMENDOUS PROGRESS, VERONICA," Dr. DeLucchi said with a smile on her face. She didn't smile often, so I knew I'd earned it.

"But I still feel like shit. All I can think about is how this new guy isn't into me."

"I warned you that, at times, healing will feel more painful than how you lived before. The difference is, you're experiencing the pain of growth, not the pain of suffering."

"Ugh. I guess." I smiled, too. I'd noticed whether I spoke here in therapy, in meetings, or with Sadé, I described my discomfort with a smile on my face. It wasn't a façade; it was hope. I had hope now.

"There's one last area I'd encourage you to explore." I held my breath because therapy homework was always brutal before it was helpful.

"OK," I said hesitantly.

"Your relationship with yourself is improving. You're more disciplined and you're thriving as a big sister of sorts with the at-risk teens. Can you see those things?"

"Yes." I genuinely could, but where was she headed with this?

"Good. The one area you seem to feel stuck in is in your romantic relationships." My shoulders slumped. That was the understatement of the year. "I believe bringing your parents into a session could be a real challenge, but also, the missing piece for your healing moving forward."

I blinked at her. *Was she out of her fucking mind?*

"I'm not crazy, and I do mean Darnell, your birth father. Your relationship with your stepfather sounds as stable as the one with your mother. But the effect of the time you lived with Darnell is still causing you pain.

"There's no hurry to take on this work today. Just keep it in mind. As far as I'm concerned, your work with me is done."

"What?" She'd just suggested I confront the man who abused me in childhood, now I'm done. *What?*

"I intend to email the dean, saying you have completed the counseling necessary to finish your time at ENEP after the session with your parents. You are not a risk to yourself or others. I'm so proud of you and I hope you're proud of you, too."

Before I could stop myself, I'd rushed over to Dr. DeLucchi and gave her a tight hug.

"Thank you, Dr. DeLucchi. Thank you for everything."

I left with a feeling of accomplishment in this area of my life. As I waited for the elevator outside of my therapist's office, I thought about how much I needed a vacation. I wanted relief from ENEP and my obsession over where I stood with Big Nate.

I'd taken a break from social media, but felt like I was kept in the loop from the group chat with my sorority sisters. Lisa was the main one to send GIFs, links, and tea. I offhandedly mentioned I wanted to get away in the chat, and Lisa replied to my message with an all-inclusive deal for a trip to Cabo. Evidently, there were students who posted about the sales on social media.

I'd spent another weekend all by myself. I missed Nate, but I couldn't sit and waste away. I booked a flight and hotel from inside my car in the parking garage of Dr. DeLucchi's office without a second thought. It was a rash decision, and thank God, I already had a passport. This would be the last weekend alone in my little apartment. I was headed to Mexico in eight days.

MEXICO WAS EXACTLY the change in scenery I needed to shake myself out of my small funk. Maybe it was the ocean side, over-sized lounge chairs, or the warmth of the sun against my skin. I couldn't be sure of the reason, but I felt free. I lathered myself with sunscreen and drank water between sips of my fruity, alcoholic drink.

I spoke with my mom, read a little of my book, and took a nap. I wondered if three days would be enough time here. I turned to my left and saw what looked like Nina. *What a small world!*

Once I was sure it was her, I lifted from my chair and walked over to hers.

"Nina. It's me, Veronica."

She reflexively placed her hand over her not-so-small belly, and I cleared my throat.

"Oh, I didn't recognize you with short hair," she spoke quietly with a look of uncertainty about what the hell it was I wanted.

"I, uh... I won't take up too much of your time. I wanted... I needed to apologize for what I did."

She placed her other hand over her heart. The sight of her there with her pregnant belly exposed and open to a conversation with me was indescribable. I couldn't believe I was responsible for one of the most painful experiences of her life.

"I'm not supposed to speak to you or Rashad, but I wanted to tell you that you didn't deserve for me to violate your privacy the way I did. I would take it back if I could." My eyes misted, but I held the tears back. This moment was not about me; it was about an acknowledgment of my problematic behavior and the harm it caused the maternal goddess seated in front of me.

"Wow. I'm speechless."

"You don't have to say anything."

"Thank you," she said to me as tears streamed down her face. I felt awful to see tears in her eyes. I'd taken a special moment between her and Rashad, the father of her child, and tainted it by posting it across social media.

"I know your ass is not in my woman's face!" Rashad's shrill voice scared both of us.

Nina struggled to get up. I assisted her and I guess it confused Rashad. He ran up to me like he would actually hit me.

"Baby, she apologized." She grasped his arm, and I saw him visibly relax. "She didn't have to. She couldn't have known we were here, but when she recognized me, she came over to make peace." Nina turned to face me. "Thank you, Veronica. I wish you nothing but love and happiness."

As if that wasn't enough to make me regret my actions, she leaned over and pulled me into an embrace. Nina hugged me tightly and I felt nothing but loving energy radiate from her.

"I suggest you make peace with her, too, handsome," Nina said to Rashad. She gave me one last smile, then waddled away from us.

Rashad and I stood awkwardly without a word for what felt like forever.

"I wasn't going to hurt her Rashad."

"I don't know what the hell you might do," he growled.

"I deserve that. I've changed, but I don't expect you to see or acknowledge it. I'm sorry for how I hurt Nina and how it indirectly hurt you."

"Indirectly—"

"OK. I did try to break you up and I almost succeeded. I only said indirectly because when you got back together with Nina, I know seeing her hurt must've hurt you. I'm sorry, Rashad, and I'm glad to see you happy with Nina."

He regarded me silently before allowing a small smile to break across his face.

"Thank you for saying that and for apologizing to her. It means a lot."

"Of course." We stood a little less awkward, but now without the tension.

"So did you and Tony make it official or... It's none of my business. I don't even know why I brought it up."

"Rashad, it's fine. Tony and I aren't a thing. I actually fell for D's play brother, Nate."

"Oh, snap! No wonder. I called you a few choice names and he laid my ass on my back. Said I needed to learn to speak better about women." We shared a cordial laugh. I didn't expect to be good friends with Nina or Rashad, but I felt so much better to know there was no more animosity.

"Congratulations on the baby. You're gonna be a great father."

"You really think so?" Rashad's face lit up at the mention of his future child.

"Of course." I hit him playfully on the arm, and he pulled me in for a quick hug. His body was unexpectedly jerked away from me. Nate seemed to appear from out of nowhere and had Rashad in a full nelson before either of us knew what happened.

"Nate, what are you doing?" I yelled. "Let him go."

He loosened his grip and Rashad shoved him forcefully in the chest.

"Check your man, Veronica," Rashad said and stormed off.

"What the hell is your problem?" I asked Nate with my hands on my hips.

"What the hell are you doin', talking to your ex with your titties out?" he whisper-yelled at me.

"You have some nerve."

"What the hell are you talking about, Chantel?"

I sucked in a breath at the sound of my name on his angry lips. He was always fine, but mad Nate was downright mouth-watering. But I wouldn't let myself be distracted by the thump between my legs. We needed to get a few things cleared up first.

"I'm talking about you being hugged up with Zanaé less than forty-eight hours after you prayed over my pussy. I'm talking about you not responding to my calls or texts and you looking caught in the act at your villa with a cute, young girl.

"You like fucking students, Nate? You had me worried I'd get you in trouble, and there you were, with a smaller, younger chick at your apartment."

He scratched the back of his head, and I wanted to yank his hand away. I was so annoyed. What the hell was there for him to consider?

"Zanaé has a man. He was there on campus, and I would have introduced you to everyone if you weren't so insecure."

I turned to storm off because, fuck this. Before I could make it far, his hands were on me. I turned to face him with my hands crossed over my chest.

"What?"

"OK. I can understand the jealousy, but why take the call from whoever the fuck Tony is? And why are you in Cabo, hugged up with Rashad?"

I dropped my head. "You're right, taking a call from Tony was a mistake. I'll give you that. But can you explain why you didn't pick up my calls? And why you had another girl at your place?"

He chuckled. "That wasn't a girl, that's my baby sister."

Before I knew what happened, I slapped him and I didn't feel bad about it. *And you shouldn't!*

"Veronica, what the—"

"No. You purposely didn't disclose she was your sister because what, you were testing me? Fuck you, Nate." This time, when I stormed off, I didn't look back. *To hell with him!*

Seventeen

NATE

I'D LOST my cool when I saw Veronica in Cabo, hugged up with Rashad. *What the hell was she doing here?* It didn't look like she'd come here to follow me; she looked shocked to see me at all. After I admitted Talley was my sister, she lost it. Her expression sliced through my heart and I knew instantly I'd pushed her too far. *Why hadn't I just told her Talley was my sister?* Maybe I was testing her and that shit wasn't cool.

When I saw her with Rashad, she had on a teeny ass, bright orange bikini with a brown mesh coverup. I was a hypocrite for overreacting after I'd accused her of doing the same when she saw me with Zanaé. I wanted Veronica badly, and not because I thought she might still be interested in Rashad. I liked her and I wanted to claim her. I just had no idea how to make things right at this point.

I made a few calls and took D's advice to throw around my title. I felt slimy as hell, but got the information I needed as far as where Veronica stayed. I rushed over to her resort and thanked Black Jesus I knew friends in high places.

I knocked on her door until she finally opened it. She'd changed into a green beach dress with exposed skin from her neck to below her belly button. There was flimsy fabric that wrapped around her neck and barely covered her breasts. The dress was fitted around her waist by a belt and the splits up to her hips were visible because she wore heels on her tiny feet. I think she was naked underneath. She held a clutch in her hand like she was on her way out. *The fuck?*

"Hell naw," I said as I stepped in and closed the door behind me.

"How'd you know where to find me?" she asked, deadpan. She sounded like I had pushed her too far. *And where the hell was she headed?* It was not like I expected her to be in her room, crying. *Yeah, you did!*

"You going somewhere?" I gritted my teeth because she better not be here to meet another man.

"Why does it matter to you, Nate? If I would have called you before you thought you saw me flirting with my ex, would you have even answered? Exactly." She walked around me and picked up her hotel key card.

"Come here." Veronica stopped and turned to face me. She didn't come to me like I'd asked, with her sassy ass, but she stayed. "I'm sorry."

"Whatever." She turned toward the door again, and this time, I had to stand in front of it to block her from leaving.

"You lost your mind if you think you taking your fine ass out the door wearing that." I growled at her.

"You don't own me, Nate. You made it clear you were no longer interested in me."

I grabbed her by the neck firmly. Her moan in response to the pressure made my dick jump. I'd already told her once I entered her, she belonged to me, but it looked like she needed to be reminded. I kissed her so deeply, she lost her balance. I scooped her up into my arms and her legs automatically wrapped around me. I had to have her. I missed her.

I turned us so that her back was against the door.

"This is my pussy, Chantel. Did you forget?"

"No."

"Tell me."

"No."

I walked her to the bed and laid her down gently. I lifted the chiffon material and growled angrily when I found she wore no panties underneath. When I glared up at her, she smirked. I yanked her to the edge of the bed and placed my face between her thighs.

"You belong to me, baby. This pussy belongs to me." I slurped and I kissed and I licked until her legs shook uncontrollably.

I quickly undressed and covered myself with protection.

"Can I have you?"

She nodded.

"Tell me, baby. I need to hear it. Can I have you?"

"Yes, Nate."

I fucked Chantel Veronica like my life depended on it. All the things I didn't have the words for, I said it with my body. I wasn't the slow grind type of man, but I did some of that to show her how much she meant to me. I wanted her in my life, and I'd make sure she'd know it before she left this resort.

THE NEXT MORNING, I opened my eyes to brightness within a room I didn't recognize. I wasn't drunk, but I'd had a few shots before I found out where her room was. I was in Veronica's room. However, she was nowhere to be found. I lifted slowly so I could orient myself to my surroundings. Her green dress was on the floor, at the side of the bed, but her sexy body was not.

I sat at the edge of the bed and called out to her.

"Veronica." No answer.

I stood to find the bathroom to take a piss, and when I'd finished my business and washed my hands, I heard the hotel door open. Veronica was in skimpy workout gear and sweaty like she'd done a morning run.

"Damn, I missed you," I said before I could stop myself.

"I was only gone for an hour."

"No, I mean, I missed not talking to you."

"I don't understand you. I may have acted jealous, but you're giving me mixed signals, Nate. And just because you fucked me and you keep claiming my body, doesn't mean much if you're unable or unwilling to communicate."

Damn, she is sexy! I'd spent so much time convinced she was the immature one, I'd messed around and missed my own childish ways.

"I'm sorry I didn't pick up your calls or respond to your texts. I'm also sorry I didn't tell you about NaTalley, my baby sister. I apologize for not reaching out to you about Zanaé. I could have made it clear to you the nature of our relationship."

"Which is?" She looked so cute when she was all sassy and assertive. *Damn!*

"I worked with her and her team on some legal stuff and things worked out in their favor. They came to campus to thank me."

"Why the hell did she have her hands on your face and around your neck?" I walked over to her, dick swinging. She tried not to look, but she did. "You can't keep using your body to deflect from mature conversations, Nate."

"My body distracting you, Chantel?" She sucked in a breath but rolled her eyes. "OK, I'll be serious. I want to show you something. Come here."

"Can you put on a towel or something first?"

"Yeah, baby. Not a problem." I swiped a towel from the bathroom to cover myself and walked over to my pants to grab my phone. "This is for you."

"Veronica," Zanaé started. Her flawless face appeared on my phone on a video I begged her to make for Veronica. Veronica's eyes widened. "Girl, you have a good man in Nathaniel Brown. He helped me out with legal advice and spoke so highly of you. I wanted to meet you the day we were on campus, but I understand; my man is always telling me I'm too friendly. Nate showed me a video from your social media, and girl, you can sang!" Veronica whipped her head to face me, but no words came out.

"I heard you work with at-risk girls and, if you'll have me, I'd love to come and dance with them or teach them something new. And if you're up for it, maybe we could sing something together? Let me know what you think, so my team can set it up. And if you haven't already, lock Nate down before somebody else gets him." The video ended and Veronica held my phone without saying a word.

"You OK?"

"I love you. I mean, I love it," she said with the most innocent smile I'd ever seen.

"I love you, too. I mean, it, too," I replied as I lifted her so her ass rested on my forearms. "I love you, Chantel Veronica Waters. Would you go with me?" We burst into laughter. "I'm gonna need an answer, baby. And don't worry about me getting into trouble. I spoke with President Reed. He wasn't happy about it, but he respected that I brought it to him first. He pulled my name from your case, and he says he has my back if anything goes down. Like I said, will you go with me?"

She giggled and responded, "Yes, Professor Brown. I'll go with you."

Epilogue

VERONICA

IT HAD BEEN three months since I'd returned from Mexico, and the professor became my man. We barely left my resort once we made things official. When I was at my lowest, shortly after my arrest, I binge-watched TV series and romantic comedies incessantly. I think I may have conjured some of the same magic in my real life.

Nate was thoughtful in public and determined to keep up his record of giving me no less than two orgasms each time we had sex. I told him I didn't care as long as he put in work in the bedroom, but he looked at me like I had five heads.

The professor worked a lot, which didn't bother me at all. I wouldn't want to wear out my welcome, and I preferred a man who didn't want to be up under me day and night.

I accepted a full-time position with the at-risk girls. I'd maintain my status as a volunteer until after graduation. They liked me, but I became the coolest person in the world when I took Zanaé up on her offer to visit. The two of us taught them a dance and sang them a song. It made the news and I'd gotten offers from several talent agents.

For the time being, I declined. I was content with the life I had. Of course, it was a huge stroke to my ego to go viral for something positive for once, but I didn't need to be a singer to be good enough. I was sure of it now.

Life on campus was mellow and I rarely got negative comments or hate mail. I did get glares of disapproval from Professor Walker, but she was just salty Big Nate was wrapped around my finger. I told him to tone it down on campus with the ass grabs and neck kisses, but the man had a mind of his own.

I'd even been signed off by Dr. DeLucchi. At her suggestion, I attempted to explore the state of my relationship with my father. I looked him up, but he wouldn't take my calls. He hung up in my face when he realized who I was.

I asked Dr. DeLucchi if we could continue our sessions around my daddy issues because I had no fucking clue what to do about any of it. It hurt my feelings that he'd rejected me, and I couldn't help but wish I still only had hate in my heart for him, but I genuinely wanted him to want a relationship with me. Now that Dr. DeLucchi and those meetings had melted my bad bitch exterior, I needed help with acceptance of his rejection.

Nate said he had big news for me, and I hoped it was to tell me he'd convinced his baby sister Talley to stay. We'd become good friends, and except for Sadé, I didn't have very many genuine girl friends in my life. Even Lisa had been on her best behavior. She talked about how she'd officially made an agreement with herself to only date men no one else in her friend circle knew or had known. I was proud of her and glad to still have her in my life.

I headed to D's apartment to pick NaTalley up so we could go to her brother's villa. I was comfortable at D's place, whether Rashad and Nina were there or not. It was much easier to see them and Nina's growing belly. We were all cordial, and it was more than I could have asked for.

I pulled up to D's house in the Lincoln and he ran outside to make a big deal about it.

"Aww, shit! It's a wrap when a man lets you drive his car. When LaTonya started driving mine, we were engaged a few months later, nah mean?" D's loud voice boomed through the open window.

"Whatever." I blushed. "Where's Talley?"

"She inside somewhere. Y'all going to see Nate?"

"Yep."

I made my way into D's apartment and heard talking in the kitchen. I figured LaTonya or Rashad had company of their own. D's apartment always had people in and out of it.

"Why don't you come visit me?" a voice I didn't recognize said.

"I just got here. My brother and D will kill you if they know we messed around," Talley whispered. I heard kissing sounds. I was slow to cover my mouth before I gasped. *Who was Talley messing around with? Was it someone I knew?*

The voices lowered and I heard shuffling. Talley stepped out first, and right on her heels was Rashad's military friend, Kadeem.

Epilogue

NATE

I COULDN'T WAIT to tell Veronica I'd accepted a full-time law professor position at ENEP. I was nervous because, though I'd make more as a professor, the assumption was teachers were broke. Veronica might like the idea of me practicing law here, but I was a different person when I prepared for trial and things were too new with us, so I didn't want to chance it.

Thanks to D, I had investments and properties in Ohio, and soon, I'd have one in Cali. It wasn't like I was hurting for money, but Veronica deserved the best, with her spoiled ass. The thing was, there was nothing I enjoyed more than giving her whatever she wanted and a few things she didn't.

I needed to decide if I would renew my lease at the Utopian Villas soon. I hoped Veronica would agree to either move in with me or let me buy us something new altogether. A bigger place would give us enough room for Talley to visit comfortably.

Talley was another reason I was hesitant about my news. What if she hated it here? I knew she liked to visit, but what if she didn't want to live in California or leave Mom and Dad? I couldn't blame her. But ultimately, my plan was to get her here, then Mom and Dad.

I heard my car pull up and my big ass got butterflies in my stomach.

I'd fallen for Veronica hard and I legit gave zero fucks who had an issue with it. Rashad, Tony, Professor Walker; they could all suck a dick. I was cool if I had to be around Rashad, but I liked his homie Kadeem a lot more. He'd been around for an extended leave. Whenever I went to D's and the two of them were there, I inevitably ended up in an in-depth conversation with Kadeem.

I opened the door and noticed Veronica's demeanor was off. Talley wouldn't make eye contact with me, and I instantly knew something went down.

"Everything OK baby?" I asked, as my eyes bounced between them.

"Hey, professor." She leaned up and kissed my lips. I forgot to be suspicious about anything.

"Get a room," Talley said as she brushed by us to enter the villa.

"What's up with her?" I asked with my hands all over my lady.

"Girl stuff. What's this big news you have?"

"I wanted to tell you together, but I don't mind telling you."

"What is it? You're freaking me out." Her eyes were wide, and I was tempted to keep her in the dark on purpose.

"I took a full-time gig at ENEP." I held my breath because we hadn't discussed any future plans. We'd decided to be exclusive, but that was all.

She stood as if to weigh my words, and I felt like my heart would pound a hole through my chest in anticipation.

"I bagged a professor?" She smirked up at me and I lost it. I grabbed her, and like always, she wrapped her legs around my waist.

"Hell yeah, baby. You're OK with it?"

"Why wouldn't I be?" she asked, with her lips less than an inch from mine. I saw her beautiful face up close, and I'd never been so content in my life.

"I don't know. People assume I won't make as much money teaching as I could if I practiced law. I also didn't know where things would go between us or if you wanted me to stay."

"You're crazy as hell if you think I don't want you here with me. And I use Google; you're not making pennies." She smiled at me with a devious look in her eyes.

"I love you."

"Yeah, I know you do."

"I want to talk about Talley, professor." I walked her to my room and closed and locked the door.

"You know how distracted I get when you call me professor." I laid her on my bed and lowered my body on top of her so I could plant kisses on her lips and across her freckles.

She moaned and tried unsuccessfully to regain her composure. "I think you want to know about what's going on with your sister."

"It can wait, baby, let me claim you."

"You already did, professor."

"There you go, talking that shit. Tell me you belong to me."

"I belong to you, professor."

"Tell me you love me."

"Make me," she purred.

I didn't want to fuck my woman's brains out with my baby sister in the house, but she'd forced my hand. I had a few ideas on how to make this sexy, sassy student comply, and I'd do it for as long as she allowed me to.

THE END

Afterword

Dear Reader,

Thank you for finishing Book 3 of the College Route.

If you enjoyed Veronica and Nate's story in *The Visiting Professor*, leave a positive review on Amazon, without spoilers, please, and share it with your friends.

Also, be sure to show my Facebook like page some love with a like and follow!

https://www.facebook.com/DeniseEssex222

Thank you in advance,
Denise Essex

Afterword

Connect with me for more of my work!
With Love, Denise Essex

Book 4 of the College Route is coming early 2023! Sign up for my mailing list to learn whose story is up next.
Also, if you'd like to read a few deleted scenes or sneak peeks, sign up for my mailing list

Mailing List: http://eepurl.com/h15QoD
Readers Group: https://www.facebook.com/groups/deniseessexheat-seekers
Amazon Author Page: https://www.amazon.com/author/denise_essex
Facebook page: https://www.facebook.com/DeniseEssexAuthor
INSTAGRAM: https://www.instagram.com/deniseessex222/
@DeniseEssex222

Made in the USA
Columbia, SC
01 January 2025

50949260R00085